THE MAN WHO KNEW
CHARLIE CHAPLIN

Other Books by Eric Koch

FICTION

THE FRENCH KISS
McClelland & Stewart, Toronto, 1969

THE LEISURE RIOTS
Tundra Books, Montreal, 1973
German paperback version, Die Freizei Revoluzzer, *Heyne Verlag, Munich*

THE LAST THING YOU'D WANT TO KNOW
Tundra Books, Montreal, 1976
German paperback version, Die Spanne Leben. *Heyne Verlag, Munich*
(Both German versions were reissued together in 1987 under the title C.R.U.P.P.)

GOOD NIGHT, LITTLE SPY
Virgo Press, Toronto and Ram Publishing Company, London, 1979

KASSANDRUS
Heyne Verlag, Munich, 1988
Liebe und Mord auf Xananta *Eichborn Verlag, Frankfurt, 1992*

ICON IN LOVE: A NOVEL ABOUT GOETHE
Mosaic Press, Oakville, 1998
Noblepreis fur Goethe, *Fischer Taschenbuch 14536, Frankfurt, 1999*

NON-FICTION

DEEMED SUSPECT
Methuen of Canada, Toronto, 1980

INSIDE SEVEN DAYS
Prentice Hall of Canada, Toronto, 1986

HILMAR AND ODETTE
McClelland & Stewart, Toronto, 1996

THE BROTHERS HAMBOURG
Robin Brass, Toronto, 1997

THE MAN WHO KNEW
CHARLIE CHAPLIN

A NOVEL ABOUT THE WEIMAR REPUBLIC

ERIC KOCH

Mosaic Press

OAKVILLE ON - NIAGARA FALLS NY

Canadian Cataloguing in Publication Data

Koch, Eric, 1919-
    The man who knew Charlie Chaplin

ISBN 0-88962-718-5 (bound) ISBN 0-88962-719-3 (pbk.)
1. Chaplin, Charlie, 1889-1977 – Fiction. 2. Hitler, Adolf, 1889-1945 –Fiction.
I. Title.

    PS8521.O23M36 2000   C813'.54   C99-932884-0
    PR9199.3.K616M36 2000

Photo of Charlie Chaplin reprinted, by permission, from Roy Export Company Establishment.
Photo of Jacob Gould Schurman reprinted, by permission, from Cornell University.
Photo of Herbert Hoover reprinted, by permission
Photo of Lili Deutsch reprinted, by permission, from Professor Ernst Schulin, Freiburg.
Photos for Walther Rathenau, Ernst Toller, Harry Domela, Bernhard Weiss, Paul Levi, Kurt von
Schleicher, Albert Einstein, Kurt Tucholsky reprinted, by permission, from Ullstein Bilderdienst, Berlin.
We regret that our determined efforts to obtain permission for the remaining pictures alas, proved
fruitless.

Published by MOSAIC PRESS, P.O. Box 1032, Oakville, Ontario, L6J 5E9, Canada.
Offices and warehouse at 1252 Speers Road, Units #1&2, Oakville, Ontario, L6L 5N9,
Canada and Mosaic Press, 4500 Witmer Industrial Estates, PMB 145, Niagara Falls, NY
14305-1386

Mosaic Press acknowledges the assistance of the Canada Council, the Ontario Arts
Council and the Department of Canadian Heritage, Government of Canada for their
support of our publishing programme.

Le Conseil des Arts | The Canada Council
du Canada | for the Arts

MOSAIC PRESS, in Canada:
1252 Speers Road, Units #1 & 2,
Oakville, Ontario, L6L 5N9
Phone / Fax: 905-825-2130
mosaicpress@on.aibn.com

MOSAIC PRESS, in the USA:
4500 Witmer Industrial Estates
PMB 145, Niagara Falls,
NY 14305-1386 Tel:1-800-387-8992
mosaicpress@on.aibn.com

TABLE OF CONTENTS

Photos ix

Author's Note xvi

Preface xvii

Introduction xviii

Chapter 1: Bärbl's Author 1

Chapter 2: Peter in the White House 6

Chapter 3: On Board S.S. *Samaria* 13

Chapter 4: The Arrival 17

Chapter 5: Brigitte 25

Chapter 6: Rathenau 35

Chapter 7: Red Berlin 44

Chapter 8: Peter in Love 54

Chapter 9: Margarete 61

Chapter 10: The Phony Prince 70

Chapter 11: Peter's Generous Host 80

Chapter 12: Isidor 87

Chapter 13: A Telegram and a Visit 94

Chapter 14: The Last Chance 98

Chapter 15: A Political General 107

Chapter 16: Die Grüne Katze 114

Chapter 17: Einstein 122

Chapter 18: Die Fledermaus 127

Chapter 19: Das Romanische Café 133

Chapter 20: The Report 143

Chapter 21: A Letter from Dr. Bernhard Weiss 146

Notes 150

Providence was in an ironical mood when, fifty years ago this week, it was ordained that Charles Chaplin and Adolf Hitler should make their entry into the world within four days of each other. Each in his own way has expressed the ideas, sentiments, aspirations of the millions of struggling citizens ground between the upper and the lower millstone of society.

The date of their birth and the identical little moustache (grotesque intentionally in Mr. Chaplin) might well have been fixed by nature to betray the common origin of their genius. For genius each of them undeniably possesses. Each has mirrored the same reality—the predicament of the "little man" in modern society. Each is a distorting mirror, the one for good, the other for untold evil.

In Chaplin the little man is a clown, timid, incompetent, infinitely resourceful yet bewildered by a world that has no place for him. The apple he bites has a worm in it; his trousers, remnants of gentility, trip him up; his cane pretends to a dignity his position is far from justifying; when he pulls a lever it is the wrong one and disaster follows. He is a heroic figure, but heroic only in the patience and resource with which he receives the blows that fall upon his bowler. In his actions and loves he emulates the angels.

But in Herr Hitler the angel has become a devil. The soleless boots have become Reitstiefel [riding boots]; the shapeless trousers, riding breeches; the cane, a riding crop, the bowler, a forage cap. **The Tramp has become a Storm Trooper.**

Only the moustache is the same.

The Spectator, London
21.4.1939

ACKNOWLEDGEMENTS

I would like to thank my friend, the perfect publisher Howard Aster, for rejecting the first versions of this book and for not accepting it until he was satisfied, and my perfectionist daughter, the copy editor Madeline Koch, for being a severe disciplinarian.

Otto H. Kahn

The Kaiser

Hindenburg
President of the Weimar Rebublic

PRESIDENT HERBERT HOOVER
(CHAPTER 2)

JACOB GOULD SCHURMAN
(CHAPTER 4)

LOUISE BROOKS
(CHAPTER 5)

WALTHER RATHENAU
(CHAPTER 6)

LILI DEUTSCH
(CHAPTER 6)

Ernst Toller
(chapter 7)

Charlie Chaplin in the 1920's
(chapter 8)

Charlie Chaplin in *The Great Dictator*
(chapter 9)

HARRY DOMELA
(CHAPTER 10)

HJALMAR SCHACHT
(CHAPTER 11)

DR. BERNHARD WEISS
(CHAPTER 12)

PAUL LEVI
(CHAPTER 14)

GENERAL KURT VON SCHLEICHER
(CHAPTER 15)

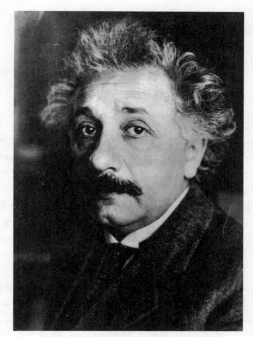

ALBERT EINSTEIN
(CHAPTER 17)

KURT TUCHOLSKY
(CHAPTER 19)

AUTHOR'S NOTE

This is a book of fiction. However, a few readers with long memories may note a remote resemblance between my invented central figure, Peter Hammersmith, and a real person, the financier and philanthropist Otto H. Kahn (1867–1934), born in Mannheim, a partner of the New York banking house Kuhn, Loeb & Co., with which he was associated for thirty-seven years.

Otto H., as he was usually called, is best remembered as the saviour of the Metropolitan Opera in New York when it was in financial trouble early in the century. He became a stockholder, made good its losses and became its guiding light. In 1908, he brought in Arturo Toscanini from La Scala in Milan. He was president from 1918 until 1931.

Kahn also wrote a number of books on art, finance and politics. His sister, Lili Deutsch (1869–1940), was a close friend of Walther Rathenau, the German foreign minister who was assassinated in June 1922. She is an important character in this novel. In order to avoid too close an identification, she is called Gertrud.

Lili Deutsch survived her brother and died in the spring of 1940 while fleeing to the United States, under circumstances that are not entirely clear, with her daughter and son-in-law, the conductor and musicologist Gustav Brecher, a protégé of Richard Strauss. According to one version, the ship that was taking them from Belgium across the Atlantic was torpedoed.

There is no evidence that Otto H. Kahn knew Charlie Chaplin. But already before 1914, partly because of the success of Chaplin's short films, Otto H. foresaw that investors could make a great deal of money in Hollywood. He was in touch with a number of motion picture producers, among others with Adolph Zukor, the chairman of the board of Paramount Pictures. In 1928 Kahn was elected to the board.

In that year Kahn visited the West Coast and met Cecil B. DeMille who showed him his *King of Kings*.

"I had twenty-five hundred extras in that one scene," De Mille boasted. "What do you say to that?"

"Nothing," Kahn replied. "Have you ever seen Velasquez' *Surrender of Breda*? That canvas looks as though it has twenty-five hundred soldiers in it, but when you count the spears, you find that there are exactly eighteen of them. And that, Mr. De Mille, is art!"[1]

PREFACE

In the fall of 1929 Peter Hammersmith, the flamboyant Wall Street millionaire and philanthropist, went to his native Berlin on a political mission for his friend President Herbert Hoover. There, as usual, he kept a diary and made detailed notes of his conversations, hoping that they might become the raw material of a separate book. He died before he could write that book.

Since his arrival in the United States in 1904 at the age of twenty, Peter Hammersmith had kept a diary, not for any private purpose but with the declared intention to have it published. He was rightly proud of his powers of observation, his judgement in financial, political and artistic matters, and of his literary style. By 1929 three volumes had appeared. They are now considered an invaluable record of the history of the United States and Germany in the early part of the century.

His wife, Catherine, who died recently, did not wish his Berlin diary to be published in her lifetime. She saw no reason to make it known to the world that during his last trip to his native city her husband had an affair with a young UFA actress. His children and grandchildren have no comparable reservations and understand that, in relation to the extraordinary historical content of the diary, the story of the love affair is insignificant, even though a curious aspect of it, by no means insignificant and at first glance inexplicable, was that Peter's lover had reminded him of the American star playing Lulu in G. W. Pabst's silent movie *Die Büchse der Pandora* [Pandora's Box]. Moreover, they were intrigued by the connection, however indirect, between the love affair and Charlie Chaplin. They had no objection to the publication of excerpts from the diary, together with the notes he took for a separate book on his Berlin mission.

INTRODUCTION

Peter Hammersmith knew that his rivals called him a publicity-hungry dandy, but he did not mind. He knew that his prowess as an analyst of market trends, and his prescience generally, had enabled him to become a Wall Street millionaire within two years of his arrival in America, and to increase his assets by a factor of two to three every year in the twenty-five years since then. By 1914, after his marriage to Catherine, he owned a townhouse on Fifth Avenue, at the corner of Ninety-First Street, and a turreted château, modeled on the French Renaissance castles along the Loire, at Cold Spring Harbor on the North Shore of Long Island, near the Phippses, the Whitneys and the Vanderbilts. Orson Welles used a stock shot of it in *Citizen Kane*.

The dining room seated two hundred people, but usually the guests were limited to fifty. There were two elevators and three staircases. The estate included a fifteen-hole golf course. The château had hundred and twenty-six rooms and employed hundred and twenty-seven servants. These were looked after until the end of their days. 'Being a Hammersmith pensioner,' Catherine used to say, 'gives you everlasting life.' His endowments to the Broadway theatre were legendary, as was his support of innumerable writers and actors.

Peter had strong political interests and many friends in Washington. He was a true-blue Republican and contributed funds to the campaigns of Warren G. Harding and Calvin Coolidge, and in 1928 he gave a considerable sum to that of his old friend, now the new President Herbert Hoover. In 1922 he was persuaded to run for municipal office on a Republican ticket but changed his mind at the last minute when he decided that his political advisers had been wrong and that, after all, a millionaire with a strong German accent had too many strikes against him, so soon after the war.

Peter saw nothing contradictory in being a Republican in the United States and a supporter of the moderate Left in Germany.

Photographs of his agreeable round face with the kindly, twinkly eyes often appeared in the press, and his blazer and straw hat in the summer, his fur coat in the winter, and the pink pearl in his Parisian silk ties all the year round, were easy to spot whenever he appeared in public. He was close to the Algonquin Round Table, with the result that his name appeared so often in *The New Yorker's* Talk of the Town columns that at one point Harold Ross, the editor, posted a note on the office bulletin board: 'Peter Hammersmith has been mentioned six times in Talk recently. There will be no more mention of him for six months.'

His ability to anticipate what was going to happen was legendary. Sometimes he was asked whether he had come to America in 1904 because he knew that the Kaiser was going to start a war in Europe ten years later, and whether he had also foretold that Germany would lose it. He would answer no, by no means—this had become clear to him only in 1912, not any earlier.

Peter did not tell anybody that he also suspected the war would go out of control as soon as it had started. He just had a hunch, but he never talked about his hunches. He had a hunch that the German generals who would talk Kaiser Wilhelm into starting a war would not have the slightest idea that, even if they would win it—which he knew they could not—it would put an end to the only world they knew and the only world they considered worth living in.

There was only one way to prevent war, Peter thought in 1912. There would be no war if England made a last-minute effort to persuade the French and the Russians to cooperate with them in convincing the Kaiser and the generals around him that they had no intention to encircle Germany, that the Germans should stop being so paranoid, that they had only friendly intentions and that they were quite willing to compete with Germany peacefully. But that was asking for too much.

Peter had suspected for some years that a war might be welcome to the top people in Germany because it would provide them with an opportunity to crush the rising tide of left-wing opposition to Prussian militarism that threatened their hold on the country. In January 1912 the Social Democratic Party became the largest in the Reichstag. He had often observed that it was always news to Americans to discover that there was a strong social democratic tradition in Germany, deeply rooted in the romantic nationalism that had inspired the revolution of 1848. He often added, when the subject came up, especially after 1914, that the Kaiser and his government regarded members of the opposition as traitors.

• • •

The charmed life of a millionaire with the golden touch was in sharp contrast to Peter's anguished, rebellious adolescence in Berlin, his Sturm und Drang period. It coincided with the fin-de-siècle when decadence was in high fashion. He never quite grew out of it, appearances notwithstanding. He was an enthusiastic reader of Nietzsche, Ibsen, Strindberg and Wedekind, of symbolist poets and avant-garde playwrights fighting Victorian hypocrisy, prudery and bourgeois smugness. He always remembered the first time he read Wedekind's play *Frühlings Erwachen* [Spring's Awakening], which precisely met his own condition. He was fourteen at the time. The subject was the anguish of sexual awakening and the denial of natural instincts that society, committed to the repression of Beauty and Truth, regarded as sinful. Later he was similarly thrilled when he read Wedekind's two explosive Lulu-plays, *Der Erdgeist* [Earth Spirit] and *Die Büchse der Pandora* [Pandora's Box]. He remembered that Wedekind described Lulu as the embodiment of primitive sexuality, a woman innocently unaware of the lethal damage she did. Six lovers—five men and one woman—die because of her, until in the last scene Jack the Ripper slices her up in an attic in London's East End.

Peter grew up in a high-ceilinged apartment on the Pommersche Strasse in Berlin-Wilmersdorf, near the Emser Platz, and went to the Fichte Gymnasium. He had more reason to complain of his elderly parents' distance and lack of understanding than of any actual repression. His father, Friedrich Hammerschmidt, a senior functionary in Prussia's Ministry of Forests and a solid upholder of Bismarck's Germany, and his mother Sophie, an accomplished piano teacher, were well meaning but remote. Both died in the 'flu epidemic of 1919.

Peter's sister Gertrud, her mother's prize student, was fifteen years older than he, so much older that she was more of an aunt than a sister. He never became close to her. His parents were proud of her beauty and, in 1893, of her marriage to the unusually able and ambitious industrialist Felix Deutsch, who was eleven years older and also a great music lover. She was twenty-four at the time, and Peter nine.

Gertrud and Felix had been introduced by mutual friends during an intermission at a Beethoven concert of the Berliner Symphoniker, conducted by Hans von Bülow. Felix was the son of a cantor in Breslau. Peter was pleased to note that if the Hammerschmidt parents objected to their daughter marrying a Jew, they did not show it. In his youth Felix sang an aria from *Die Walküre* at a public concert under the direction of Richard Wagner himself. He quickly rose in the ranks of the Allgemeine Elektrizitätsgesellschaft, the A.E.G., one of Germany's largest industrial empires and the biggest electro-technical group. Felix worked closely with the founder, Emil Rathenau, whose career was launched when he saw Edison's light bulb at the Paris Electricity Exhibition in Paris in 1881 and a year later bought the patents after long, difficult negotiations.

Emil's son Walther, Felix's rival and friend, was a hugely ambitious, dominating, vain and immensely complex celebrity with whom Gertrud had formed a deep friendship lasting fifteen years. It began in 1907 and ended with Walther's assassination in 1922, after he had become, for five months, foreign minister.

The assassination of Walther Rathenau was a turning point in the history of the Weimar republic.

He had been an outstanding industrialist and a best-selling, idealistic and future-oriented writer on social, political, economic and philosophical subjects. He had also been the administrator of raw materials during the first year of WWI.

His position before 1914 was compared with that of a monarch. It seemed—and he wanted the world to believe—that he knew everybody, not only in Germany but also in France and England, and in many other countries. He had traveled widely, even in Africa, and had a highly developed social conscience. However, it was characteristic of him that he was intensely uncomfortable in the presence of members of the lower classes. It was fortunate for him that such occasions were rare.

Rathenau had occasional but substantial conversations with the Kaiser. One of these took place on February 13, 1912, when the Kaiser's told him about his idea of forming a United States of Europe to compete with America. This was an idea which was close to Rathenau's own thinking at the time. The Kaiser had confided this concept to his cousin King George V. The English, the Kaiser told Rathenau, were by no means unsympathetic.

• • •

Considering Gertrud's and Peter's conventional, undistinguished background, it was truly remarkable, and a testimony to their enormous gifts, that both Hammerschmidt children would reach the pinnacle of society, one in Europe, the other in America.

No doubt Peter would have become a millionaire had he stayed in Germany. As a matter of fact, he would never have gone to America had he not had a crush on Margarete Schulenberg, who believed in free love and played Lulu in a private amateur performance of Wedekind's *Earth Spirit*. (The censor did not allow public performances.) After graduating from the gymnasium in the spring of 1904, Margarete sailed to New York with an older cousin to spend the summer with a rich American uncle.

Peter had just finished his military training in Küstrin. With only mild objections from his parents, he spent a substantial part of his paternal grandfather's inheritance to purchase a return ticket on the S.S. *Aquitania* and followed her.

To Peter, Margarete was indistinguishable from Lulu, an innocent femme fatale who acted instinctively and was incapable of rational thought. For Wedekind, and for Peter, sex provided the only honest means of communication between men and women in a society trapped in a web of lies.

Once in New York, Peter took a room in the Hotel Astor on Times Square. It was equipped with a large double bed, in which Peter and Margarete spent many afternoons together, totally honest with each other. Since Peter knew the Lulu-plays inside out, he was sure he was psychologically protected from lethal consequences.

Margarete's rich American uncle, her mother's brother, was Jim Lawrence, who together with Thomas Tyler owned the banking house Lawrence and Tyler on Wall Street. They specialized in assembling and managing security-purchase syndicates, for which they usually charged a fee of one percent. They were also leaders in railroad reorganizations, and were particularly known for their lucrative practice of purchasing the depreciated shares of distressed railroads, which, after they reorganized them, rose steeply. The percentage received by each partner depended on seniority, the volume of business he engendered, and other considerations.

Margarete introduced Peter to her uncle, who invited him to dinner. Lawrence immediately recognized the young man's talents. The next day he asked Peter if he would like to come to his office for a few days and observe what was going on. Peter was delighted. He was a quick study. He made a few calculations in his head and made three suggestions that enabled the bank to make an immediate profit of $500,000. Lawrence promptly offered him a job. Peter accepted, cashed in his return ticket and changed his name from Hammerschmidt to Hammersmith. After three months Margarete and Peter decided it was time for a change of lovers but they would always remain friends. She returned to Berlin.

Peter's success was dazzling. Prescience is invaluable on Wall Street, especially when coupled with rare mathematical gifts, great personal charm and, towards the outside world, a sunny disposition. In 1906, Jim Lawrence took Peter to Washington to show him off to his friend President Teddy Roosevelt, the first of three presidents Peter was to meet. Peter did not quite share Mr. Roosevelt's enthusiasm for Kaiser Wilhelm, but he did not yet predict a war.

In 1909, Peter became a partner at Lawrence and Tyler, which entitled him to 28 percent of the bank's annual profits, calculated according to the business he brought in. In 1910, he married Lawrence's daughter Catherine, who never found out about his affair with her cousin Margarete.

He went back to Berlin every year for business reasons and to visit his parents, and Gertrud and Felix, as well as Margarete, who in the meantime had married a young doctor, his old classsmate from the Fichte Gymnasium, Teddy Lindhoff.

During his visit in 1912, he had an experience that convinced him that war was overwhelmingly likely. (He always avoided the word 'inevitable.') Discussions between Germany and England about a naval agreement had just broken down. But that was not the reason. After all, talks could always be resumed. The reason was that in a café on the Pariser Platz near the Reichstag he overheard a conversation between two newly elected social democratic deputies. Usually social democrats voted against the government's military budgets. Still, these two coffee-drinking Marxists used crudely jingoistic anti-French and anti-Russian language, the Kaiser's language, so paranoid that he decided if and when the Moment of Truth came they would vote for war. They said nothing about the English. The Kaiser, too, a grandson of Queen Victoria, was usually ambivalent about them. If this kind of suicidal insanity has spread to socialists, Peter thought, Imperial Germany was doomed.

By now he was a fervent American patriot. Once war broke out in 1914, he went around the country making speeches about German militarism and the opposition to it, and raising funds for Belgian war relief, in conjunction with his old friend Herbert Hoover. Early in 1918, he went overseas to talk to French and English troops at the western front. Some one told him afterwards that German intelligence had found out about the trip and that the Kaiser himself had ordered his U-boots to torpedo his ship because he considered the Berlin-born American millionaire more dangerous than General Pershing.

Peter was strongly opposed to a vindictive peace treaty motivated by emotion rather than reason. On January 15, 1920, he was a signatory, together with his friend Herbert Hoover, William Howard Taft, and J. P. Morgan, Jr., of an appeal authored by John Maynard Keynes and Paul Warburg, stating that burdensome reparations could foster revolution in Germany and Austria. The Germans and Austrians would simply print money to outwit their former enemies. Keynes considered reparations as 'morally detestable, politically foolish and economically nonsensical.'

In November 1918, after Germany's capitulation, Peter was pleased that the social democrats formed the new government. During the chaotic days following the abdication of the Kaiser they thought that their most important task was to prevent a Bolshevik revolution of the kind that had occurred in St. Petersburg only a year earlier, after a similar collapse. Peter could not have agreed more. The idea of communists seizing power in Germany had been a nightmare to him since October 1917, and he agreed with the socialists that the new revolutionary government should do everything possible, including mobilizing the paramilitary Freikorps [Free Corps], which were strictly forbidden by the Allies, to put down the Bolsheviks.

In March 1920 Peter made a personal donation of $2 million to a special fund designed for help finance anti-Bolshevik activities. Five years later he was told that $100,000 had been left over and was invested in the publication in Munich of an obscure book written by a bumbling, right-wing adventurer who, in November 1923, had made an amateurish attempt in a Munich beer hall to take over the government, and was now no more than an almost unknown, marginal figure in German politics. This was of no great interest to him. He simply shrugged and said, "What a waste of money!"

The book was *Mein Kampf*.

1

BÄRBL'S AUTHOR

As Peter was going upstairs to the library of his château on Long Island, in a splendid mood after Dorothy Parker, George Gershwin and a
few hung-over survivors of Calvin Coolidge's Treasury Department had
departed, one of his one hundred and forty-seven servants, Bärbl, was gathering ashtrays. Breaking his rule never to talk to the staff unless absolutely
necessary Peter said, "Hello, Bärbl." He happened to remember her name
because he liked to speak German to her. Or rather, he spoke German, she
spoke Bavarian. Bärbl came from Munich. He liked her freckles.

Excerpt from Peter's diary:

Sunday, October 6, 1929
"Have you heard anything from home recently, Bärbl?" I asked her.
"Oh, yes, sir," she said. "I had a letter from my brother yesterday."
"And what did he say?"
"He was all excited, sir. He's just joined some sort of boy scouts.
They go out in the woods and sing songs."
"How nice," I said. My attention was wandering.
"They all wear lovely brown shirts," Bärbl burbled on, "and have a
leader who has a little black moustache and has written a book. My
brother sent it to me."
"Oh? A Bavarian boy scout who's written a book? How peculiar."
"Would you like me to show it to you, sir?"
"Oh, no thanks, Bärbl, please don't bother."

1

"It's no bother at all, sir. My brother says it's probably the first copy ever to cross the Atlantic. But it won't be the last, he says. It's all about politics. I don't know why he wants me to read it. He knows very well I'm not interested."

"All right, Bärbl. I'll take a look at it."

I had hoped at last to begin reading *The Magic Mountain*. Groucho Marx mentioned at dinner last night that Thomas Mann was going to receive this year's Nobel Prize for Literature. But I dipped into Bärbl's book, it won and Thomas Mann's lost.

I do not know why I was so slow, but it did not dawn on me when I started reading that this was the book in which I had accidentally invested $100,000. This only occurred to me after I had reach page 5. I froze with horror. I was paralyzed.

Oh, what have I done! How could I, the man who has been dining out for years all over New York and Washington on being right about the future, not have known in 1920 that by endowing a fund dedicated to fighting Bolsheviks I was not only financing honorable activities to promote Democracy and Capitalism, Freedom and Justice, but also the kind of person who wrote this book? It is beyond belief.

I went on reading. Never before had I held in my hand a book quite as anti-human, as barbarous, as vulgar, as repulsive, as loathsome, as monstrously immoral as this one. It was abominably written, pompous, bloated, inflated, demagogic, self-dramatizing, disorganized, maddeningly repetitive and far too long. Still, its inherent power, conviction and, given the author's assumptions, consistency held me spellbound. How could any person believe this? I kept asking myself. But I could not deny that there was a certain logic in his thought.

I would imagine few people could read it through, from beginning to end. I certainly could not. All I could do was skim it and read and reread certain sections, horrified. My only hope was that the book would be quickly forgotten, and was merely one of hundreds such works that would never come my way.

But suppose I was wrong? Suppose it would turn out to be important, after all? That was the question I asked myself again and again.

Why did it take me so long to think of the answer? The book would only become important if its author became important. In itself it could do no harm. No book can, by itself. (Nor can any book do any good, by itself.) What harm to Rome would Martin Luther's theses on the church door of Wittenberg have done if it had not been for the circumstances, for the moment? This author was clearly unable to write a readable book, but that might be irrelevant. He might very well have other talents. Now, what did I know about him? Oh yes, I was told four years ago that he was a bumbling, right-wing adventurer who, in November 1923, had made a clumsy attempt in a Munich beer hall to take over the government. Now that I came to think of it, I had heard other things as well. He was apparently an electrifying, mesmerizing speaker. Perhaps he had political, strategic gifts as well, though this was extremely unlikely, to judge by his performance at the bungled putsch attempt. On the other hand, I remember reading that this man—his name was Adolf Hitler—gave such an impressive performance at his trial for high treason that one of the judges exclaimed 'What a tremendous fellow, this fellow Hitler.' And I also heard that after his conviction he spent less than a year in the comfortable fortress-prison of Landsberg, in the company of many of his disciples, where he wrote the book. Or rather dictated it to one of his men. I even remembered reading about the author's sarcastic expression of gratitude to the state for providing him with a higher education.

• • •

Peter knew a horrific bank crash was in the offing, followed by a devastating depression. It seemed to him inconceivable that the Weimar republic could survive. Until the moment he read the book he assumed that, once this happened and democracy in Germany collapsed, the event he had been dreading all these years would occur and the communists would take over. But now he changed his mind. Something even worse would happen. Bärbl's author would be the man to whom the Germans would flock, not the communists, after the forthcoming collapse had taken its toll and there was massive unemployment and misery. After four years of trench warfare and millions of dead, after the traumatic humiliation of Versailles, after the devastating inflation, Adolf Hitler would be the man of the hour and take over the government, by hook or by crook. He was definitely a stronger candidate than any of Stalin's followers in Germany. After all, Hitler's loyalties were to Germany, not to Russia. If Peter was right, this would be an ever greater catastrophe for Germany and the entire world than a communist Germany. Hitler would most certainly provoke another world war. *Mein Kampf* could not be more specific on that point. The communists prefer mere civil wars.

However, nothing was inevitable until it happened. Peter would have to do everything he could to prevent this horror. The first thing to do was to talk to his old friend Herbert Hoover.

Notes

"This man could not be more ambitious," I told Catherine at dinner, referring to Bärbl's author, but, naturally, not confessing my substantial role as accessory to evil. "Compared to him, the Kaiser was a raw amateur. This man thinks in terms of destiny, of divine predetermination. He is the messiah leading the world into a new era. Nature, he says—or, alternatively Providence—has determined that Germany, as the main habitat of the noble and biologically superior race of Aryans, will rule the world. He happens to be an Austrian, but to him Austria and Germany are the same. All non-Aryan people must be subservient to the prerogatives of the biological elite, the Aryans. Any obstacle that stands in the way of Nature's obvious intentions has to be removed, above all mankind's, not merely the Aryans', universal enemies, the Jews. They alone bear the responsibility for the decline and corruption of the world. They use both Capitalism and Bolshevism as their means to dominate it for their diabolical purposes. They are parasites who contaminate all other races with their poison and have to be dealt with the way parasites are dealt with. The sacred service Germany has to render to the world is to liberate mankind from their deadly grip."

"Peter, you're ruining my dinner," Catherine said.

I ignored her.

"Nature intends the superior race of Aryans to be unpolluted," I continued. "The mixture of races thwarts Nature's intention and therefore cannot be tolerated.

"Russia has natural Lebensraum, living space, for the German race. A foreign policy has to be devised accordingly. No treaty needs to be kept unless it helps achieve Nature's aims. Germany is the arena in which the future of mankind will be decided.

"Bärbl's author worships force and has nothing but contempt for those who don't. He says the masses are like a woman who would rather submit to a strong man than dominate a weakling.

"The clear implication is that the strong man is to be the author himself, but he never spells this out.

"In his vocabulary it is good to be fanatical and bad to be humane and compassionate. That is a sign of weakness.

'Who,' he asks, 'is guilty if the cat eats the mouse?'"

2

PETER IN THE WHITE HOUSE

Peter had retained Wedekind's fin-de-siècle view of the heavy odds, in this sadly imperfect world, against ordinary people being able to lead honest and fulfilling lives. He did not believe that man was capable of devising a society categorically different from the one in which he lived. Peter's religion was art and literature—and beautiful women who were usually, but not always, tolerated by his worldly-wise wife Catherine, the mother of their two teen-age boys.

No one could have been more different than Herbert Hoover, who was ten years older. It was remarkable that for more than twenty years they had been such good friends. The first time they met was in 1908 when Peter's career as a millionaire was only beginning, while the future president's as an entrepreneur who owned profitable mining operations in the United States, Asia and Africa was already in full swing. Both were bargainers of unusual shrewdness.

Herbert Hoover was a Quaker, the first Quaker president of the United States, the son of a small farmer and inventor in Ohio. He was an optimist, a practical idealist, a believer in education and voluntarism, a puritanical activist and reformer who, unlike Peter, firmly believed in human progress. Living in the Far East had strengthened his conviction that western technology and rationalized methods of work could be of immense benefit to non-western societies. He never strayed from his marriage vows.

When Hoover attended the Peace Conference in Paris in 1919 as U.S. Food Administrator, Peter sent him a telegram to encourage him to speak out against the French, who insisted on a tough, vindictive treaty. Keynes said Hoover was the only man who emerged from the ordeal with an enhanced reputation. He thought Hoover's hard-headed moralism was an effective antidote to the abstract rhetoric of President Woodrow Wilson.

When Hoover was Secretary of Commerce in Coolidge's administration Peter had a good deal to do with him in connection with the massive loans he was negotiating with German industry and municipalities. In 1924 Hoover recommended Charles Dawes, the president of the Central Trust Company of Illinois, to head a commission that lowered reparation payments substantially. This was the Dawes Plan, which Peter supported firmly. Dawes received the Nobel Peace Prize in 1925, together with Sir Austen Chamberlain, the British Foreign Secretary.

In 1929, at the time Peter read *Mein Kampf,* the Dawes Plan was superseded by the Young Plan, named after Owen Young, the chairman of General Electric. It reduced the payments further. Those payments were to last until 1988. But first it had to be ratified by the Reichstag, a matter hotly opposed by Adolf Hitler and sections of the Nationalist Party.

Peter was soon to find himself in the middle of the debate.

Excerpt from Peter's diary:

<u>Thursday, October 10, 1929</u>

This was our first meeting since H.H. took office in January. Of course I called him 'Mr. President.'

How the White House has changed! He employs three secretaries instead of one, which was quite enough for Warren Harding and Calvin Coolidge. Not only that, but each of the three secretaries now suddenly has to have a separate office, plus a small room for a stenographer! Washington has gone wild! What a change since 1906 when old Jim Lawrence took me here to show me off to Teddy Roosevelt.

I hardly remember my second visit to the White House early in 1918. That's when Woodrow Wilson consulted me on the economic situation. Maybe I can't remember the visit because W.W. was a Democrat.

While in the Oval Office before H.H. arrived I inhaled the aroma of his cigars as I looked out through the French doors to the autumnal Rose Garden.

My gosh—we've been friends for a whole generation!

Naturally the first thing we talked about was the market. I told him

I was predicting a severe crash, any moment now. H.H. said he antici-pated it, too, and to soften the effects he was doing all he could to reduce the size and extent of stock market operations. As a matter of fact, already two days after taking office in January, he said, he had conferred with Federal Reserve officials to persuade them to take ac-tion to reduce stock speculation. When he was still Secretary of Com-merce, he had said that the banks were ignoring the domestic conse-quences of easy money at their peril. That was four years ago. He had warned them that this was bound to lead to a collapse. Fortunately, today the economy was strong enough to recover quickly.

I did not agree at all, and said so.

Notes

I told the president I saw a long depression coming. It would spread all over the world.

That stopped him.

"I guess I should listen to you, Peter," he said, lighting a cigar. "I remember people used to say you were psychic. Your predictions always turned out to be right."

"By no means," I hastened to reply. "But I keep quiet about the occasions when I'm wrong."

"I don't believe it," he laughed. "When people said you were psychic I usually told them you were merely smarter than everybody else. Before 1914, you went around town and told everybody the Germans suffered from persecution mania and felt they were being encircled, and that it was up to us to tell the English and the French to take the greatest care not to provoke them. You said the Kaiser was always trying to prove that he was as good as his cousin the King of England, but that you were very pessimistic because even some German socialists were talking the Kaiser's crazy language. You went around the country saying so, at your own expense. You spoke with a German accent about your native country, so every-body understood that you knew from your own personal expe-rience what you were talking about. You raised funds for a systematic campaign to prepare us to join the Allies the mo-ment it became necessary. You made sure that your speeches were published and distributed across the country. Many of your friends on Wall Street were furious with you. They preferred the Germans to the British and the French. And certainly to the Russians. But you always remained very much attached to your native country. Even though you were proud to have become an American. And then, once the war started, you predicted that by 1917 we would be drawn in. Didn't everybody on Wall Street tell you to shut up?"

"They certainly did."

"Now tell me what you have on your mind."

"Mr. President, have you ever suffered from the unintended, unpleasant consequences of something you've done of which you had been proud?"

He looked at me, frowning. "Oh, I'm sure. Let me think. In 1919, against everybody's advice, I allowed food to be sent to Hungary while Lenin's friend Béla Kun was in power. The result was Béla Kun soon felt strong enough to execute hundreds of first-class people. Why are you asking?"

I told him about donating money to an anti-Bolshevik fund, thereby helping the publication of a terrible book by a man called Adolf Hitler. Certainly an unintended, most unpleasant consequence for which I felt responsible. Though of course I knew this feeling was entirely irrational. But I couldn't help it. I told him what I knew about the man. I sketched his background and summarized his book. I was terrified, I said, and told him he met many specifications of a great popular leader in times of crisis. Even being an Austrian rather than a German might be an advantage. I explained that he would appear to be not an ordinary, conventional politician but a saviour, a redeemer who'd arrived from outside, selfless and incorruptible. His message would be ideological, almost spiritual. At the same time he might convince the electorate that he was a man of the future, that he was committed to technological progress, that he had a grand vision but had his feet on the ground. I gave the president my reasons for believing that the forthcoming crisis might create conditions that would enable Adolf Hitler to come to power and ultimately drag Germany and the whole world into another war. Anger and hunger, and a profound sense of humiliation, might make many idealistic Germans support him because he would appeal to their patriotism, to their sense of order. He might convince them that he could lead them out of the intractable mess the Treaty of Versailles had caused, that he could erase the clause attributing guilt for the war to Germany alone, which, he would argue, had been designed to create a moral, if not a legal basis for exacting crushing reparations. He might conduct a vigorous campaign against Marxists, and claim that his was the natural party for German working men, not the Moscow-dominated communists. Germany never lost the war, he would say, but had been stabbed in the back by Marxists and Jews who committed high treason when they surrendered, for their own reasons, and then later signed the Treaty of Versailles. At first he might underplay his anti-Semitism, in order to give priority to his promise of national regeneration. He might deliberately leave open the question what he would do to purge Germany of the Jews, an intention he had clearly stated in his book. But who had read it? Many people might think his anti-Semitism was merely conventional rhetoric and didn't mean very much. They would find out later that it was absolutely fundamental to him and that he could not be more serious about it. His appetite for power might be greater than that of any of his rivals and he might be able to outmanoeuvre them easily. They would wake up one morning to discover he had become chancellor, legally or illegally. At first they would think they could manipulate this talkative, low-class charlatan for their own purposes. Luck might very well favour him. He would quickly abolish the constitution, destroy the opposition, use propaganda with unprecedented effectiveness and—in a manner not seen in western Europe since the days of Robespierre—terror. Sacred ends would justify ruthless means, even against rivals in his own party, against old enemies and against anyone able to threaten his power base. At the same time, he would see to it that his party was well organized, that its members were friendly and helpful to those who supported it, that they were good neighbours and they might actually mean it. In this way he might gradually consolidate his power. He might try to conceal his real purpose, which would be to rearm and start and win another war. Outside observers, however, would very quickly look through this masquerade. It would become clear that the powers that crushed the Kaiser would once again have to join together in order to stop him. Timing would be of the utmost importance. Obviously, the sooner they acted, the better.

H.H. listened to me with signs of growing impatience. But he did not interrupt.

"This is one of the times when you're wrong, Peter," he said when I was finished. "You're persuasive as usual and you paint a compelling picture. But you're wrong. Being a former German yourself you're too close to the scene to see the situation clearly. We're talking about the best-educated people in the world. Our universities are modeled on their universities. You and I had no use for the Kaiser. But he's no longer in the picture. The way you describe this man, this half-crazed fanatic, this semi-literate rabble-rouser with a typewriter and the gift of the gab who's not even a German—no, Peter. This time you're wrong."

I was silent.

"Germany has made tremendous progress," H.H. went on. "Its real social production is now higher than it was in 1913, before the war, reparations notwithstanding. Yes, I know Gustav Stresemann's death last week was a terrible blow, but I'm told there are many other good people who can carry on his work."

As chancellor and as foreign minister Gustav Stresemann had done more than any other Weimar politician to achieve reconciliation between Germany and the Allies.

I remained silent.

He blew smoke rings to the ceiling.

"When were you in Berlin last?"

"In the spring."

"Can you go again, right now, and talk to the brightest people you can find for a couple a weeks, and report back to me? Find out what they think of this man who's thrown you off balance. How they assess the situation."

"I'd be happy to do that, Mr. President."

"Many of the leading people you know already. Didn't you have a sister there, who'd been a friend of the foreign minister who was assassinated?"

"Yes, I do. Gertrud. She was a friend of Walther Rathenau. What a good memory you have, Mr. President."

"You once introduced me to her, in Lausanne, I think. I remember her well. Very handsome woman. And I think you've had dealings with the president of the Reichsbank who got the credit for ending the inflation. I've forgotten this name. He has an unusual first name."

"Hjalmar Schacht."

"Oh yes. Hjalmar."

Anyway, I'll ask Hughes to contact our ambassador there, Jacob Gould Schurman. Former president of Cornell. You'll like him. He's a philosopher. He can suggest a few people you may not know."

"I've met him, Mr. President. You're right, he's a good man."

Hoover accompanied me to the door.

"Write your report first while you're still in Berlin," he said. "Send it to me through the embassy. Once you're back home come and see me and fill me in on the details."

"I shall be honoured to do that, Mr. President."

3

ON BOARD S.S. *SAMARIA*

Headlines in the *New York Times*:

Thursday, October 24, 1929

12,894,650 SHARES SWAMP MARKETS

LEADERS CONFER, FIND CONDITIONS SOUND

WALL STREET OPTIMISTIC, AFTER STORMY DAY

• • •

Friday, October 25, 1929

WORST STOCK CRASH STEMMED BY BANKS

• • •

Saturday, October 26, 1929

STOCKS GAIN AS MARKET IS STEADIED

BANKERS PLEDGE CONTINUED SUPPORT

HOOVER SAYS BUSINESS BASIS IS SOUND

TRADING IS NEAR NORMAL

Excerpts from Peter's diary:

<u>Thursday, October 24, to Saturday, October 26, 1929</u>

At the captain's table they all lied and said they saw it coming. I also lied, to make them feel better, and said I was surprised. Nobody dared to ask me how much I lost.

Afterwards, in the lounge, I played my usual game, carefully scrutinizing the German passengers, trying to guess what they were up to. It's a game I cannot lose since I don't ever expect to be right. Being obsessed with Germans, I ignore non-Germans.

The little man with the gold-rimmed pince-nez, talking to the grandmother-type in the grey dress, was on Prinz Max von Baden's staff and went with him to Supreme Military Command in Spa in occupied Belgium on November 6, 1918, to tell the Kaiser he had to abdicate.

The girl with the horn-rimmed glasses who looks like a small town librarian is the daughter of Philipp Scheidemann, the social democrat who, on the spur of the moment, carried away by the emotion of the moment and without any authority whatsoever, proclaimed the German Republic from the steps of the Reichstag on November 9.

The hollow-cheeked character with the severe cough is the second cousin of Gustav Noske, the social democrat who, two weeks later, as Supreme Commander, at the request of his friend the President of the Republic, Friedrich Ebert, used the Army to put down radical revolutionaries.

The ample-bosomed matron in the dark-brown dress, just ordering her third brandy, is the mother-in-law of any one of many monocled Reichswehr generals who, in return for hard cash, made arrangements for German pilots to train in Soviet Russia, behind the back of the Allies but with the tacit consent of the German government.

The white-haired lady talking to what appeared to be her granddaughter is the secretary of Wilhelm Marx, the candidate from the Catholic Centre Party who ran against Field Marshall Hindenburg in the presidential election of 1925, and received as many as 13.7 million votes, as against Hindenburg's mere 14.6 million. (I'm amazed I remember these numbers.)

The imitation Kaiser over there, with the high collar and the up-turned moustache, and the shrill drill-sergeant's voice that can be heard all over the lounge, is a judge of a high court in Hanover.

The young man behind the potted palm shamelessly flirting with an American beauty is an interpreter who in 1925 accompanied Foreign Minister Stresemann to the Locarno conference where Germany, France and Belgium guaranteed the existing borders and promised to refrain from any attempts to alter them by force of arms. No doubt he also accompanied Stresemann to Geneva, where Germany was reluctantly admitted to the League of Nations. The young man was probably among the millions who cried at Stresemann's funeral three weeks ago.

• • •

Went for a stroll on A-Deck with Emma Eberstein, the elderly theatre and movie critic of the *Berliner Anzeiger*, the woman with the most wobbly double chin in Berlin. We passed rows of passengers, covered in blankets in spite of the mild weather, happy to be able to enjoy the S. S. *Samaria's* (prepaid) ample food and drink while they still could.

Emma Eberstein was on her way home after inspecting Marc Connelly's *Green Pastures*, and Broadway's first *Uncle Vanya*. I did not tell her that I had financed them both. Of course she could only see a fraction of this season's New York's two hundred and thirty-three productions. I always like her crisp reviews, invariably written in short paragraphs, like the Criminal Code. Last year, when I heard about Ibsen's *Ghosts* at the *Staatstheater* with Fritz Kortner and Lucie Höflich, I asked Gertrud to send me Emma Eberstein's review.

Notes

> I asked Emma Eberstein about the Emil Jannings film they were shooting at the UFA studios in Neubabelsberg—a film version of Heinrich Mann's novel *Professor Unrat*, which came out in 1905.
> "I believe they're still rehearsing," she said. "Shooting will

begin next week. They're calling it *The Blue Angel*."

I wanted to know who was playing the girl.

A young lady, she said, calculated to trigger a sexual earthquake.

Hm.

I ask whether that's what the UFA press release said.

Her double chin wobbles when she laughs. No, regrettably she had not seen any UFA press release on the subject. Nor had she seen the Trojan press release when Helen launched a thousand ships. The young lady's name was Marlene Dietrich. The director Josef von Sternberg and the producer Erich Pommer spotted her on the stage in September in a play called *Zwei Krawatten* [Two Ties] by Georg Kaiser. Hans Albers was the star. She played an American millionairess and had only one line, 'May I invite you all to dine with me this evening?'

"No earthquake."

"Not yet."

"I want to meet her," I announced.

"Nothing easier. Phone me the moment you arrive."

4

THE ARRIVAL

As a boy growing up in Berlin, Peter always hated it when his uncles and aunts praised his 'sunny disposition.' What do they know, he whispered to himself, of the Sturm und Drang, the tortured anguish, the impatience, the longing, of his inner life, the need to shake off the bourgeois yoke, of his unfocused sexual urges?

At the turn of the century he was sixteen, a devotee of *l'art pour l'art*—addicted to the French symbolists, worshipping decadence and mannerism, seething with rage about what English 'cant' was doing to Oscar Wilde, whose Dorian Grey he loved. He found in the early expressionist Frank Wedekind a perfect reflection of his own psychic state and was fascinated by Wedekind's femme fatale, the anti-logical, irrational Lulu. Richard Strauss' Salome, a direct descendant of Lulu, was imminent. So was, a little later, Dadaism. Surrealism was around the corner.

What a contrast to the outer world of imperial Germany, the thrusting upwards towards what the bombastic, strutting Kaiser called 'a place in the sun,' a man lacking even the slightest inkling of the absurdity of his poses.

Nothing symbolized his nouveau riche Germany more dramatically than the Adlon Hotel, the address of which was Unter den Linden 1, on the Pariser Platz, facing the Brandenburger Tor. The Kaiser had it built in 1907, largely out of his own pocket, three years after Peter had left for America, intending it to become more lavish—and having more *Kultur*—than any hotel in London or Paris. After all, none of these had a Goethe Hall, as the Adlon had, which was only fitting in the newest hotel in the capital of Poets and Thinkers, a capital striving to become Europe's most exciting. Which indeed it did become—this was one history's more amusing ironies—a few years after the Kaiser's humiliating abdication.

It was a measure of Peter's worldliness, curiosity and sense of adventure, once he had worked out his Sturm und Drang and channeled his enormous energies and exuberant imagination into his financial and artistic enterprises, that like most moneyed Americans he invariably stayed in the Adlon when he visited his native city, especially after the war. He definitely preferred it to the more banal and pedestrian Eden Hotel, near the Zoo, which was to become the location of Vicky Baum's and Greta Garbo's Grand Hotel.

Excerpt from Peter's diary:

<u>Sunday, October 27, 1929</u>

The bellhop who took me to Room 422 after Gertrud dropped me off was agreeably talkative. He told me in the elevator that the gorgeous lady in the lobby wearing a strand of pink pearls was Natasha Fodorowitsch, the ambassador-at-large for Stalin, adding that she was talking to the Maharajah of Kapurthala. She was the daughter of a tsarist officer, he explained, who married a sailor during the mutiny in Kronstadt in 1917. She was having a reception tonight in Room 411. Did I want to be invited?

Of course, I said.

First I phoned the American Embassy, to make an appointment to see Ambassador Jacob Gould Schurman. Then I went to Room 411. There I met a few Russians, some conservative members of the Reichstag, a couple of French generals and their overdressed wives, the tenor Richard Tauber, an official in the office of Parker Gilbert, the American Agent-General for Reparations working under the terms of the Dawes Plan, a thick-necked German industrialist from the Ruhr who looked as though George Grosz had drawn him, and the super-polite general manager of the hotel who had been on its staff from the beginning. The thick-necked industrialist said, apparently in all seriousness, that he hoped nothing had happened to the bust of the Kaiser that had dominated the lobby until November 1918. It was modeled on the Emperor Augustus.

"It's in the basement," the manager replied with a bow.

"Waiting for the right moment to return?" a pretty girl smoking a cigarette on a long holder asked mischievously.

"As you wish, *mein Fräulein,*" the clever man replied.

Natasha Fodorowitsch was dazzling. We soon established that we had many friends in common. Sergei Diaghilev, for example, who had just died in Venice. What a terrible loss, we agreed. Why he had never succeeded in Berlin, a city he loved, she would never know.

I didn't want to ask her why there were no German communists at her party. Of course I knew the reason. They did not want to appear in public with an emissary of their Russian master. A few people recognized me and soon everybody wanted to know how much money I lost at last week's crash at the New York Stock Exchange. They seemed gravely disappointed when I said 'Not a cent' and quickly returned to a more rewarding subject, the *Sechstagerennen* [the Six-Day-Bicycle Race].

One of the German politicians told an amusing story. When, on November 9, 1918, the revolutionaries occupied the lobby downstairs, the girl at the newsstand jumped on top of a marble table and began singing *Die Internationale*. She tried to make the men join in, but none knew the words.

Now, nearly eleven years later, I went to the same newsstand to buy a copy of the Nazi daily, the *Völkische Beobachter*. I had read somewhere that in 1920 the Nazi Party acquired a run-down anti-Semitic gossip sheet, which was badly in debt and appeared twice a week. In 1923 it became a daily. One of those who financed it was Frau Helene Bechstein, the wife of the piano manufacturer, who admired Hitler and gave parties for him to introduce him to society. It carried an editorial about the 'unlawful and unconstitutional terror' that prevented many civil servants and those 'dependent on Jewish money-bags' from voting in the forthcoming plebiscite for the 'Freedom Law,' also known as 'The Law Against the Enslavement of the German Nation,' which the Nationalists and the Nazis had just introduced in the Reichstag.

On July 9, 1929, I already knew, Alfred Hugenberg and Adolf Hitler had united to form a national committee for a referendum on the Young Plan. According to Article 73, Paragraph 3, of the Weimar constitution, a popular referendum had to be initiated by the submission of a detailed legislative proposal to the Minister of Justice. A draft was submitted on September 28, a few days before Stresemann's death. The draft consisted of only four paragraphs, 'each of these,' my eloquent source told me, 'deserves a special place in any political or constitutional chamber of horrors.' It demanded the annulment of the war-guilt clause, the end of all reparations, immediate evacuation of the occupied territories, and the punishment of all cabinet ministers and members of the government aiding and abetting the 'enslavement of the German people.' It also provided for no less than two years' imprisonment as a common felon for 'any chancellor, minister of authorized agent of the state,' of which President Hindenburg undoubtedly was one, who might dare to sign treaties with foreign powers. Such a person would be guilty of treason according to Paragraph 92, Section 3, of the Criminal Code.

Endlessly repeated slogans accompanied the petition in the right-wing press. They called the Young Plan the 'death penalty on the unborn,' the 'Golgotha of the German people' whom the executioners were 'nailing to the cross with scornful laughter.' However, when the proposal came to a vote in the Reichstag it was defeated by an even greater margin than had been expected.

The *Völkische Beobachter* called the parties who accepted the Young Plan *'Terroristen-Parteien.'* Their adherents, I was reading in the copy I had just bought at the newsstand in the lobby, could not expect any consideration in the New Germany to come.

"Mister Hammersmith?"

I turned around and found myself face-to-face with a reporter, pad and paper in hand, and a photographer at his side. The hotel always lets the press know in advance when prominent people (like me!) come to Berlin.

"Rolf Uffland, *Weltzeitung.*"

I told him his editor-in-chief, Edwin Rehberg, happened to be an old friend of mine. I took the reporter to the bar and ordered two cognacs. The photographer snapped a picture and left. Uffland asked me why I was in Berlin. I told him Stresemann's death was a terrible setback. I was concerned about the immediate future, and so were my friends. So I came here for a couple of weeks to talk to a few people. I wanted to hear what they had to say.

"Do you think the crash on the New York stock exchange will affect our economy?" Uffland asked.

"I do, emphatically. It's a prelude to a long depression. This is bound to lead to a quick end of American loans. In fact, we will want our money back. That's very, very bad news for you. Your economy is in bad shape already. You've heard of the recent bankruptcies, the Frankfurter Allgemeine Versicherung, the Kieler Bank and the Südwestdeutsche Bank. By the way, Herr Uffland, have you read Adolf Hitler's book?"

"No. My time is too precious. I don't waste it on trash written by the lunatic fringe."

"Think again, Herr Uffland. In view of the forthcoming crisis he is the greatest danger the republic faces. Much greater than the communists, and certainly greater than anybody else on the Right."

"May I quote you, Mr. Hammersmith?" Uffland asked.

"You may."

Notes

The American Embassy is on the Wilhelmsplatz, within easy walking distance of the Adlon.

I first met the ambassador, Jacob Gould Schurman, last spring. I don't remember why, but he told me about growing up on a farm near Summerside in his native province of Prince Edward Island, in Canada, and about his first job at the age of thirteen as a clerk in a general store, making thirty dollars a year. He also mentioned, *en passant*, that he had nine children.

Once an academic, always an academic, even if he'd left the ranks to become, first, president of Cornell University, then, political activist and diplomat.

Schurman began by giving me a tutorial on Gustav Stresemann and the terrible loss the world suffered when he died recently.

"Did you know Stresemann and I were very close?" he

THE MAN WHO KNEW CHARLIE CHAPLIN

asked. "He was the only German present at my daughter's wedding in 1925. And last May we were both given honorary degrees by the University of Heidelberg. I spoke about the Kellogg-Briand Pact outlawing war. This was another case, I said, where the German and American governments saw eye to eye completely. You may have read my remarks in the press. I said that Germany and the United States were marching forward in 'a great and noble adventure in the cause of human civilization.' Some papers openly wondered whether our so-called 'intellectual sister act' represented the views of the State Department. To be quite frank, I didn't really care. Apparently Paris was not pleased.

"Yes, the loss of Stresemann is truly irreparable," he went on in his professional manner, but with some emotion. "Alfred Hugenberg literally drove him to his death. Did you know that he now controls five hundred newspapers, as well as the UFA? And for the last year he's also been head of the Nationalist Party, which rejects the republic and has just joined up with Adolf Hitler's Nazis to fight the Young Plan. That man has much to answer for. I suppose I should not tell you this, but I will do it anyway, that earlier this year we investigated rumours about his planning a putsch, together with some Junkers. Of course he had excellent connections, as the former general manager of Krupp, and now as one of Germany's most powerful media barons. You see, a Hugenberg dictatorship was by no means an impossibility. There was a lot of talk about Hugenberg becoming the German Mussolini. Not a very nice prospect, you must admit."

"Mr. Ambassador," I said. "You mentioned Adolf Hitler. What do you think of him?"

"He's of no consequence whatsoever by himself," the ambassador replied. "He's only important because of his new association with Hugenberg. For that reason I welcome him. He will destroy Hugenberg. Thanks to Hitler, Hugenberg's chauvinistic and irreconcilable wing of the Nationalist Party will end up in the wilderness. This will mean the end of Hugenberg in German politics and the beginning of a strong conservative party that supports the republic. You see, Herr Hammersmith, the main danger does not come from extremists, and certainly not from the communists, who are controlled by Moscow. The main danger comes from the unworkable system of voting they have in Germany. The danger is the multiplicity of parties. Already my predecessor Alanson Houghton advised our German friends to modify or eliminate proportional representation in elections for the Reichstag. I wish they'd hurry up and do it. After all, we Americans know something about such things. Still, in spite of their very bad electoral system, the republic gets stronger all the time. Its permanency can now be taken for granted."

"Even if there's serious economic trouble?" I asked. "If there's no more money coming from the United States? What will happen if there's large-scale unemployment?"

"The republic will survive," the ambassador declared firmly.

He suggested I see two people I didn't know. One on the Right, and one on the Left. On the Right, I should see General Kurt von Schleicher, who had just been appointed Chef des Ministeramts im Reichswehrministerium [Chief of the ministerial office in the defence ministry], the political liaison body between the armed services, the Reich ministries, the political parties and civilian officials. As an old friend of Hindenburg's son Oskar, he said, von Schleicher was close to President Hindenburg himself. On the Left, I should see the social democrat Paul Levi, the most eloquent political defence lawyer in Germany. A strong Marxist, he used to be a communist, a great friend of Rosa Luxemburg, whom he revered. He may even have been her lover. He was also close to Lenin until they quarreled.

I thanked the ambassador for these excellent suggestions, which, of course, I would accept. He promised to ask his staff to make the appointments for me.

• • •

Back in the hotel, Peter made his own phone calls. Eventually, this was his timetable for the next four days:

TUESDAY, OCTOBER 29
9:30 a.m.: Edwin Rehberg, editor of the *Weltzeitung*. Tour of Wedding and Neukölln
7 p.m.: Dinner with his school friend, the psychiatrist Teddy Lindhoff and his wife, Peter's 'Lulu,' Margarete.

WEDNESDAY, OCTOBER 30
4 p.m.: Reichsbank—Hjalmar Schacht, president
7 p.m.: Dinner with his school friend Bernhard Weiss,
vice-president of the Berlin police.

THURSDAY, OCTOBER 31
10 a.m.: Paul Levi, Reichstag
4 p.m.: General Kurt von Schleicher, Scharnhorst Klub.

FRIDAY, NOVEMBER 1
10 a.m.: Albert Einstein, in his apartment,
Haberlandstrasse 5, Wilmersdorf.

This seemed to him a good start. He had hoped also to see Kurt Tucholsky, the prolific left-wing journalist, novelist and writer of feuilletons, whom he admired greatly and had met several times since the war. But he was told Tucholsky no longer lived in Germany and only paid occasional visits.

5

BRIGITTE

In recent years it was one of many pleasant features of Peter's annual trips to Berlin that he invariably found agreeable lady companions to dine with, to accompany him to the theatre and to the opera, and to spend the night with him in the Adlon. Once, it was the daughter of one of his old schoolteachers at the Fichte Gymnasium. On another visit it was a member of the German Olympic fencing team, a challengingly muscular young lady whom he had met before in New York and who, when they were making love, became as soft as cotton wool and melted in his arms. On another occasion it was the black-haired cellist in the orchestra that had entertained him during dinner on the *Bremen* on which he had sailed.

Celebrity millionaires rarely have any difficulty attracting the attention of enterprising and ambitious beauties. Since Emma Eberstein had mentioned the actress designated to trigger 'a sexual explosion' as Emil Jannings' partner in *The Blue Angel*, now being filmed, he naturally hoped an encounter with her might lead to a rewarding relationship.

Her name, he remembered, was Marlene Dietrich.

• • •

From the Monday morning edition of the *Weltzeitung*:

> The prominent American banker Peter
> Hammersmith declared yesterday in an
> interview in the Adlon Hotel that he expects
> last week's crash on the New York stock
> exchange to have serious repercussions in

Germany, mainly because it will cause the end of American loans to Germany. As an informal emissary of Wall Street, he is spending two weeks in his native Berlin to assess what effect the crash could have on the political and economic situation here. He considers Adolf Hitler a graver danger to the Republic than the communists or anybody else on the Right.

Excerpt from Peter's diary:

Monday, October 28, 1929

Emma Eberstein was as good as her word. She arranged an encounter for me with Marlene Dietrich at the UFA studios in Neubabelsberg for today at four in the afternoon. A driver would pick me up at three. In the evening, Gertrud expected me for dinner.

Now that I've lived in New York for twenty-five years, Berlin once again struck me as a strangely divided city. It lacks any kind of unifying harmony. The various elements of New York have an inner relationship with one another. But the elements composing Berlin do not. For one thing, there are two totally different west ends, and a huge very poor working class east end, which people like me hardly know.

The patron saint of one of the two west ends was Frederick the Great, whose military victories turned Prussia into a major European power. At his court only French was spoken. It was only long after I had left school and come to America that I learned that this misanthropic, flute-playing and probably homosexual philosopher-king, this friend of Voltaire, was clearly no more duplicitous than his adversaries and other princes in the eighteenth century. Only he was better at the game than they were. In my youth my friends and I had always thought of him as an unmitigated ogre, just because of the official Hohenzollern hero worship.

The central artery of Frederick's Berlin was Unter den Linden, which was to evolve into one of the two west ends. There, the prevailing style is Prussian classicism, with its ideals of Duty, Virtue and Fatherland. To me, the visual expressions of these ideals, the statues of Prussian generals along the Siegesallee, seemed comic even when I was a child. They always struck me as insane aberrations. I simply could not understand how anybody with any intelligence could take them seriously, and of course most Berliners did not. Berliners are generally irreverent, disrespectful, anti-authoritarian, anti-Frederick the Great. Berlin impudence—the famous Berliner Schnauze, the Berlin big mouth—is the natural response to the Prussians' categorical imperative.

The other west end, the Kurfürstendamm, just north of my native Wilmersdorf, was then and is now the precise opposite of Unter den Linden. Here Frederick the Great's counterpart is the Whore of Babylon. The Kurfürstendamm is devoted to the pursuit of pleasure and money and to the high and the low arts and is one of the reasons why people from all corners of the universe flock here. Here sex, both normal and perverse, is open and devoid of hypocrisy, in contrast to sex in the United States. I doubt very much whether anywhere in America made-up boys parade up and down Main Street, as they do here, or whether they have many transvestite balls in American church basements where dozens of men in women's clothes and women in men's clothes dance under the benevolent eyes of the police, and I doubt as well whether in many of our side streets they perform sexual acrobatics not known to man and woman since the Rome of Suetonius, as they are alleged to do every night in the side streets of the Kurfürstendamm. I would also be a little surprised if a girl in America suspected of being a virgin at the age of sixteen would be in deep disgrace, as I'm told they are in Berlin, and if many of them boast of being lesbians.

After breakfast I performed my usual ritual when I return to Berlin. I took a taxi from West End Number One to West End Number Two. It took me down the Potsdamer Strasse, across the Nollendorf Platz, to the Pommersche Strasse 28 in Wilmersdorf, near the Emser Platz, where I was born. I went for a short stroll to the Preussen Park. At the old playground where my mother used to take me, brand-new mothers were now exhibiting their brand-new children. And on the park bench where my friend Konrad sold me a ticket at half-price for Ibsen's *John Gabriel Borkman* at the Deutsche Theater a governess was wiping the nose of a little girl. At the Deutsche Theater I first saw the young actor Max Reinhardt, whose career I've followed ever since. Konrad's favorite novelist was Mark Twain. He lent me his copy of *Huckleberry Finn*, the first book I ever read in English. When I met Mark Twain later—first in New York and then in Vienna where Twain's daughter was studying the piano—I told him that it was thanks to him that I came to America. Only fools tell the truth.

Emma Eberstein had arranged for my sexual earthquake at the UFA Studio in Neubabelsberg, near Potsdam, the most modern film factory in Europe. I was picked up punctually at three. The UFA's car was a sparkling black Maybach and the UFA's pipe-smoking driver was Fritz Wagner, who had lost his left leg in the war. The UFA's property in the treeless landscape of the Mark Brandenburg consisted of 300,000 square metres of flat land, surrounded by barbed wire. On the way, Fritz Wagner pointed out the sites—in the southwest the chimneys of a locomotive factory, in the west the suburb of Nowawes, in the northwest the gardens of the Siedlungshäuser [suburban housing], and in the north the houses of the UFA Strasse. The site itself was a complex of fairy-tale structures of odd shapes and sizes, some made of glass, connected by a network of roads with narrow-gage railway tracks and turntables.

After complying with the security formalities at the guardhouse, the pipe-smoking, one-legged Fritz Wagner showed me the costume factories, make-up rooms, photographic and camera facilities, new sound stages, painting studios, storerooms, film-processing laboratories, rehearsal halls, editing rooms, canteens and relics from the great UFA films *The Cabinet of Dr. Caligari*, *Faust*, *The Nibelungen*, *Metropolis*. We spent some time in the workshop where the tawdry cabaret set for *The Blue Angel* was being built. Painters were at work on the stage and carpenters were nailing down the trapdoor through which Marlene Dietrich would chase out the students who had come to witness their teacher's debasement. Then Wagner took me to the Administration Building where the secretary of the board, Dr. Albert Lieblich, insisted on meeting me.

Notes

Dr. Lieblich, who had been a colonel in the war, was a tall amiable man with the dueling scars of a corps student. Only the self-satirizing post-war UFA style restrained him from clicking his heels and wearing a monocle. A lawyer by training, he looked entirely plausible as a loyalist of his boss, Alfred Hugenberg. Dr. Lieblich was a living reminder that in December 1917 the Universum Film A.G. (UFA) had been founded at the instigation of General Erich Ludendorff himself, the Kaiser's deputy chief of staff and later, in November 1923, Hitler's fellow conspirator in his abortive attempt in Munich. When taking the initiative to form UFA, Ludendorff's hope was that a state-controlled, though largely privately financed, film agency could counteract Allied propaganda. On UFA's first board of directors sat carefully chosen representatives of the upper levels of imperial Germany.

I told him about my appointment with Fräulein Dietrich.

"Herr von Sternberg thinks very highly of her, Herr Hammersmith. *The Blue Angel* is, of course, very important to us. Our first sound film, you see. And Emil Jannings is a great star. Are you familiar with the story of the seductive vamp who drives the old schoolteacher to his doom?"

I said I was, and that I had just seen the set being built. As a matter of fact, I had read the novel when it first came out, just after I arrived in America. In its day, I said, it was considered a great shocker, a bitter attack on the Kaiser's Germany. Some of us young rebels loved it. The susceptible schoolteacher, I added, was a role absolutely cut out for Jannings.

Dr. Lieblich appeared interested. I asked myself whether the former anti-Kaiser shocker was a bit of problem even for today's UFA. Perhaps the moral code in today's Germany was not so different after all from that guiding the Germany of 1905. I decided not to beat around the bush and ask him directly whether the subject matter of the new film did not perhaps appear to his board a little daring.

"The board wants our management to be realistic," Dr. Lieblich replied. "The word they use is 'elastic.' Some prefer the term 'permissive.' But you're absolutely right, Herr Hammersmith. The film is very daring. The truth is we have to make money. We've had serious financial problems. It's become more and more difficult for us to compete with American films. And so many of our best directors and stars have left for Hollywood. Ernst Lubitsch, Friedrich Wilhelm Murnau, Pola Negri, Ewald André Dupont, Ludwig Berger and so many others. Fortunately Emil Jannings has come back."

"I suppose you need the revenues from export," I said.

"Oh, absolutely. Now sound will add another dimension to the problem. People hate change. Of course, many actors are against it, too, because they don't have the right kind of voice training. Now let me ask you something. Do you think this new film of ours can be shown in the United States?"

"I doubt it very much," I replied. "In spite of Emil Jannings' Academy Awards for *The Last Command* and *The Way of All Flesh*. The subject is too sordid for us. We Americans don't like that sort of thing. Too sadistic." (I enjoyed saying 'we Americans' in my Berlin dialect.) "I hope, for your sake, I'm wrong."

"So do I, I assure you, " Dr. Lieblich nodded vigorously. "I must confide to you that some members of our board are seriously worried about it for quite a different reason, nothing to do with export. The original screenplay was written by the playwright Carl Zuckmayer who was in close touch with the author of the novel, Heinrich Mann, whom he reveres. Von Sternberg then revised it, on his own, without any prompting from us. The new version is no longer a biting political satire of pre-war small-town Germany, which suits us fine, but rather a psychological study of obsession, humiliation and sexual enslavement. Heinrich Mann has seen the revised script and has approved it, perhaps reluctantly. I'm sure, like the rest of us, he hopes that appearances notwithstanding Germany is ready for this kind of film. Even if America is not."

I said I assumed the board would want to keep its distance from Heinrich Mann, a strong leftist.

"Oh yes, of course, " Dr. Lieblich smiled at me conspiratorially. "Though for the moment we don't mind at all that the Left accuses us of avoiding films with serious social content, as long as we make money. They say we make so many cheerful entertainment films"—he cleared his throat—"to 'divert the proletariat from the imminence of social revolution.' The

Right is angry that we're not German enough, in spite of all the films about Frederick the Great we're turning out."

"Would you not consider it overwhelmingly likely," I asked, "that Dr. Hugenberg's new friends will have the strongest objections to *The Blue Angel?* I mean those who together with him have just introduced the 'Law Against the Enslavement of the German Nation.'"

"You mean Adolf Hitler and his people?"

"Yes, I do."

Dr. Lieblich folded his hands solemnly and shook his head.

"Please, Herr Hammersmith, do not call them Dr. Hugenberg's friends. They're merely political allies, for a limited time, for a limited purpose. Dr. Hugenberg is a great strategist. They will be dropped, I assure you, the moment their usefulness expires."

"Have you read Hitler's book?"

"Most certainly not. I do not waste my time with such things. I cannot stand the man's primitive, vulgar, ignorant anti-Semitism. Where would UFA be without Jews? I think about a third of the members of our first board, picked in 1917 by General Ludendorff himself, were Jews. Without the Austrian Jew Carl Mayer we would never have got off the ground. I don't think Fritz Lang is a pure Aryan either, even though Hitler likes his films. By the way, so do the Soviets. Nor is Erich Pommer—the man who made *The Cabinet of Dr. Caligari*—Aryan, and he's one of our most effective producers who's also returned from Hollywood. And then there are many of our best actors and actresses, Elisabeth Bergner, Conrad Veidt, Fritz Kortner and Peter Lorre. No, Herr Hammersmith, please don't call that man Dr. Hugenberg's friend."

"I'm delighted, Dr. Lieblich," I declared, "that on my very first day back in Berlin I had occasion to hear such a reassuring speech."

Excerpt from Peter's diary:

<u>Monday, October 28, 1929</u>

Lightning struck ten minutes later. (I'm getting tired of earthquakes.) "What an amazing resemblance with Louise Brooks!" I whispered to Fritz Wagner when the breathless girl with whom I was about to fall in love nearly bumped into me in the corridor of the rehearsal building. Louise Brooks was the bewitching actress from Kansas who played Lulu— my Lulu!—in G.W. Pabst's film *Pandora's Box*. I knew, of course, that Louise Brooks was not with UFA.

"What's her name?"

"Brigitte Kerner." Fortunately she was still within earshot. "Brigitte, come here," Wagner shouted.

"Sorry, Fritz. I'm late," she shouted back.

Brigitte wore a dark green cloth coat, unbuttoned, over a simple blouse and a short skirt. Piquant. Marvelously limpid, expressive eyes. Natural grace. Pitch-black bangs, the bobbed fringe covering her forehead. *Petite*. Not at all actressy.

I smiled at her. She smiled back. Lovely dimples.

"Oh, come on, Brigitte," Wagner pleaded, putting on a big show. "This gentleman is dying to meet you."

"I know von Sternberg will whip me for this."

Brigitte had a real Berlin bedroom voice, slightly hoarse, as though she had just woken up.

"Nonsense," Wagner responded. "Nobody's going to whip you for shaking hands politely with the famous Mr. Peter Hammersmith from New York."

I knew from experience, all Berlin girls adore the sound of the words 'New York.'

Her handshake was confident, robust.

"So you're the man Dietrich is awaiting." Her expression made it abundantly clear that she could not abide Dietrich. "How do you do, Mr. Hammersmith."

"Brigitte plays one of the girls in the cabaret scene," Wagner explained.

Never mind Dietrich, I decided. Brigitte had perfect skin and the neck of a swan. Her innocent allure suggested the opposite. Lulu also looked innocent. That was the whole point.

"I understand your lovely new star is going to be a great success." I pointed vaguely in the direction where I was led to believe Dietrich was awaiting me.

"Perhaps," Brigitte pulled down the corners of her mouth. "She's certainly prepared for it. Last summer she had her nose straightened out, by a surgeon. She thought it was too Slavic. But she knows it's still no good. She hopes the director can fix it with proper lighting."

I turned to Fritz Wagner.

"Would you do me a favour, please, Herr Wagner? Would you be so kind as to have somebody tell Fräulein Dietrich that unfortunately I have to attend to an urgent business matter and am unable to see her."

He smiled. "I'll look after it right away."

"When will your rehearsal be over?" I asked Brigitte.

"At half past five."

"Will it be very much out of your way if you drive back to town with us?"

"I hope the ride lasts three hundred hours," she declared.

In the car she told me all kinds of interesting things about herself. She'd had a part in *Liebeswaltzer* with Willy Fritsch and Lilian Harvey, which no doubt I had seen. I had, but I had to confess I did not remember her. Then she talked about her director, Joseph von Sternberg. "I'm scared to death of him," she said. "Everybody thinks he's a genius, and a terrific director, and of course I shouldn't say anything because, after all, he gave me a job. But I get goose pimples all over when I see him. And not the nice, pleasant kind. I can't stand men who run around in oriental dressing gowns and riding boots. I hope you don't do that, Mr. Hammersmith."

No, I replied. I don't. We went on talking about all kinds of interesting things and then, finally, at last, I mentioned Charlie Chaplin. I said, truthfully, that Charlie was a friend of mine. That was all that was required. Now there was no longer any question, if ever there was one after I had mentioned New York and she had expressed her hope that I did not wear oriental dressing gowns and riding boots, that we were about to become lovers. The only question was when and where the affair was to begin. Not tonight, unfortunately, since I was going to have dinner with Gertrud. And tomorrow evening I was booked with Teddy and Margarete, the first Lulu in my life. Well, I was free for lunch tomorrow. Perhaps after lunch…

"Do you happen to be free for lunch tomorrow?" I asked.

She was. And not only that, she also promised to come with me to Max Reinhardt's *Fledermaus* in the Deutsche Theater on Friday.

There was, however, one tiny little detail Brigitte Kerner omitted to convey to me, of the dozens of things she did convey to me about her past and present life. She did not tell me that one of her many boyfriends was Horst Zahlendorf, the bartender in the Hotel Siegfried in Lichterfelde. In his spare time he happened to be a Nazi stormtrooper. Fritz Wagner had told me about him while we were waiting for her rehearsal to end.

The question now facing me was whether Horst Zahlendorf's leisure activity would add a special *frisson* of excitement to my forthcoming pleasures, or whether it would ruin them. Would that depend on her, on him, or on me?

• • •

The concierge at the Adlon handed Peter his key together with an envelope. He opened it. The text was typed on a blank piece of paper.

> Read this carefully, Mister Hammersmith.
> Do you want to know what happens to American millionaires who give interviews in the Adlon Hotel and tell us that they will withdraw their money unless we dance to their tune? Who use their power to enslave us?
> We will tell you, Mister Hammersmith. The age of slavery is over. Our Abraham Lincoln is Adolf Hitler. Unless you leave Berlin tomorrow your life will be in danger.

6

RATHENAU

Peter immediately called his friend Bernhard Weiss, the vice-president of the Berlin police, with whom he was going to have dinner on Wednesday. Only idiots ignore threats, he told himself. Bernhard was at a meeting. His deputy had orders not to disturb him under any circumstances. Peter put on his drillmaster's voice, which he had picked up in Küstrin while doing his military service. He barked that Dr. Weiss was certain to give him a serious reprimand if he didn't act right away.

It worked.

"I'll send you two of our most experienced men," Weiss told Peter. "Nobody can get past them. We'll talk more when we get together."

Peter knew a good deal about the incidence of political murder in Germany. He remembered a book by the mathematician and statistician Emil Julius Gumbel that had been published in 1922. It was called *Zwei Jahre Mord* [Two Years of Murder] and showed that since November 1918 there had been 318 political murders committed by the Right and 16 by the Left, and that the sentences imposed on the Right were incomparably more severe than those imposed on the Left. (Eight of the leftists were condemned to death. None of the right-wingers were.) A revised edition of the book had just appeared with the name of *Four Years of Murder*. Even the Minister of Justice agreed with Gumbel's findings.[2]

In the four years after the war, a time span that included the inflation from 1921 to 1923, 'the Right' usually meant members of the Freikorps in whom, to his eternal shame, Peter had invested $2 million, minus the $100,000 that went into the publication of *Mein Kampf*. After all, Peter was not a naïve German idealist who marched to the front in 1914 with a copy of *Faust* in his pocket. Nor was he one of those who, after barely surviving the trenches for four years, became unhinged in 1918 by the desertion of the Kaiser and the betrayal by the first president of the republic, Friedrich Ebert, the socialist who had 'sold out' to the Army to crack down on the Bolsheviks.

Peter should have known better. After all, he knew a good deal about the psyche of German nationalists. He understood perfectly well that the worship of the Fatherland was a romantic, poetic, mystical affair, not a cool, prosaic political matter. He thought that many of these worshippers believed the Fatherland had been seized by philistines, opportunists, profiteers and parasites. They had joined the Freikorps to—as they saw it—restore order, by which they meant reversing the events of 1918 and all that implied. Peter also assumed, quite rightly, that many of them had not thought this through at all and were not true believers but unemployed ex-soldiers and adventurers who had not found their way back into civilian life and had nothing better to do. But should he not also have known that they would be used as pawns by secret nationalist, counter-revolutionary organizations? Was he not famous for being unusually prescient? Was he not (nearly) always right?

Now, in 1929, there were no more Freikorps. After the stabilization of the mark in 1923, and the return of some measure of confidence as a consequence, among other things, of the influx of American capital, there had been a noticeable improvement in the economy. Many members of the Freikorps got jobs and joined the mainstream of non-radicals. Others were absorbed by paramilitary formations like Hugenberg's Stahlhelm and Nazi stormtroopers who specialized in barroom brawls and, Peter hoped, who no longer engaged in the gruesome activities that were the subject of *Four Years of Political Murder*. Today, Peter thought with grim satisfaction, he could not so easily have financed his own murder. What about commissioning a play about a millionaire who did this? After all, such a scenario would provide the essence, the very definition, of tragedy, the story of a man who unwittingly created his own doom, like Oedipus. Maybe Carl Zuckmayer, the dramatist who had adapted Heinrich Mann's *Professor Unrat* for UFA, was the man to write it.

There was one question he could not answer. Why would any disciple of Adolf Hitler want to go to the trouble of killing him, Peter Hammersmith, just because he said he considered Hitler a graver danger to the republic than the communists or anybody else on the Right? Surely he was not the only person who made that kind of mild statement, which, on reflection, nobody could call inflammatory. For that he should be killed? Why? Because his bank had given loans to the public and private sector of the Weimar republic? Berliners loved Americans and their money. Was the clue perhaps the connection so ingeniously constructed by the letter writer between Abraham Lincoln and Adolf Hitler, to remind Peter that the age of slavery was over? Did he think Peter's banking activities were attempts to enslave the German people, to force them into *Zinsknechtschaft* [interest-servitude], a word the Nazis constantly used? What was the name of the 'Freedom Law,' the bill that Alfred Hugenberg had put before the Reichstag? Was it not 'The Law Against the Enslavement of the German Nation'? Was that the key?

No, that was too absurd. Peter simply had no rational explanation. But, in contrast, there were good rational reasons why, seven years ago, when the Freikorps were still active, Walther Rathenau was chosen as a victim. Those fighters were trying to prevent the Weimar republic from taking root. They rejected it and hated it. They fought everybody who had a part in creating it and maintaining it. Rathenau had been indirectly connected with negotiations with the Allies in 1918, later with fulfilling the terms of the 'Diktat' imposed on Germany at Versailles, which included the payment of reparations. He had become a key figure among those committed to the Erfüllungspolitik [policy of fulfillment], which was designed to meet the western Allies' conditions. They saw no alternative without renewing the war, and did whatever they could to limit the damage and even to thwart Allied purposes whenever possible and when it seemed to serve the national interest. For example, as foreign minister, Rathenau made a deal with the Soviets behind the Allies' back in Rapallo in April 1922, two months before he was killed.

Peter was about to learn from Gertrud that Rathenau had changed his mind about the *Erfüllungspolitik*, for reasons that are not entirely clear, just before his death. If his assassins had known about that, they might not have gone to the trouble, on June 24, 1922, to ambush him just after he had left his house in the Grunewald, to be driven to work in the Wilhelmsstrasse, and shoot him down in the open car.

In 1922, no right-winger could, with any shadow of a justification, accuse Walther Rathenau, a fervent patriot and an industrial leader who opposed socialism, of having stabbed Germany in the back. On October 7, 1918, after Germany had officially sent a message to President Wilson requesting an armistice and subsequent peace on the basis of the President's Fourteen Points, Rathenau had written an article in the *Vossische Zeitung* opposing premature steps to make peace and suggesting 'a national defence, the rising up of the nation, a *levée en masse*, like Danton's *levée en masse* in 1793 during the French Revolution. He closed the article with the words 'It is peace we want, not war. But not a peace of surrender.'

But by June 1922 this was forgotten. Rathenau had become a symbol for coming to terms with reality. What else was the *Erfüllungspolitik?* The men in the Freikorps preferred to live in a dream-world.

Excerpt from Peter's diary

<u>Monday, October 28, 1929</u>

At seven I took a taxi to Gertrud's mansion in the Rauchstrasse, near the Tiergarten, just up the street from the Lützowplatz. She lives there alone with a cook and three maids. There was no point mentioning the letter to her. She is now an old widow of fifty-six and I didn't want to upset her. I noted with a little sadness that hers was probably one of the very few private residences in Berlin that possesses a fully grown pipe organ. Her husband Felix had it installed for the private concerts that often took place in their beautiful music room on the ground floor. He died suddenly last year. There were two portraits on the Steinway, one of Felix, one of Walther Rathenau.

Gertrud was the only one of the three or four women in his life to whom he felt a 'strong erotic attraction,' she told me two years ago. However, they had refrained from 'taking the ultimate step.' She did not tell me what she thought 'the ultimate step' would have done to her marriage—this we never discussed. In fifteen years Gertrud and Rathenau never passed from the formal *Sie* to the familiar *Du* when they addressed one another. This was perhaps not surprising because I am sure both kept their feelings under control. That was not so difficult for him because, as she once told me, he only had the desire to have feelings, not any feelings themselves. All he wanted to do was to dominate and to exercise power. I've never understood how she coped with this.

Everything about Rathenau, she said, was enigmatic. But he was endlessly fascinating for her, and for most people who knew him. I remember my first meeting with him very well. It was in 1911, during one of my return visits, at a weekend party at the beautiful Villa Deutsch in Mittelschreiberhau in the Riesengebirge, not far from their friend Gerhart Hauptmann's Haus Wiesenstein. At the turn of the century

Hauptmann, the leading playwright of his generation, had been the very antithesis of my favourite, the early expressionist Frank Wedekind (whom Rathenau also knew). But I also admired Hauptmann's gripping plays on social themes.

Gertrud had transferred her Berlin salon to the mountains. That night there were about six or seven other guests. Hauptmann was not there. I met him later. We were all drinking wine on the veranda. Rathenau spoke in a soft baritone, very compellingly. He was one of the most impressive conversationalists I've ever met. 'His mind was always on the alert,' I remember Stefan Zweig once telling me. 'It was an instrument of such precision and rapidity as I have never seen in anybody else. In speaking with him one felt stupid, faultily educated and confused in the presence of his calm, deliberate and clear-thinking objectivity.'

I remember exactly what Rathenau said when we were sitting on that veranda. 'The economy shapes our destiny,' he said, 'not politics.' I had never heard an anti-Marxist, an industrialist, saying this. Industrialists should play a greater role in public life, he said, and not leave it to Junkers, generals and socialists. In the light of Germany's immense economic progress, it was anachronistic that the men who had the greatest influence on the Kaiser were feudal barons from East Prussia, reminders of the days long ago when it was land, and not industry, that was the source of power in Germany.

Felix was used to this line of thinking. I never had any doubt that he agreed with it. But, unlike Rathenau, he was not primarily a man of profound ideas but, above all, a superlative engineer and marketing genius. Like Rathenau, he was a great German patriot, but the only thing that really moved him passionately, apart from his work, was music. The friendship he cherished most was with the relaxed and amusing Richard Strauss, who stayed with them whenever he came to Berlin and played cards with Felix and his friends till late in the night.

I asked Gertrud whether Rathenau had ever received any threatening letters.

"Oh yes, many," she replied. "He knew exactly the danger he was in. After the murder of Matthias Erzberger he offered condolences to the widow and told her he might very well be the next victim.[3] Even before Rathenau went to the conference in Genoa, the police knew of several plans to kill him.[4] At the end of May, after his return to Berlin, Chancellor Joseph Wirth came to his office, his teeth chattering. He informed him he'd had a visit from a Catholic priest. Someone had confessed to him that Rathenau was next on the murder list. Breaking the secret of the confessional lay heavily on the priest's conscience, but he later received absolution from Cardinal Pacelli.[5] Rathenau then reluctantly put himself under police protection, but he found this too irritating and countermanded it. He was fatalistic about death, but the police made him carry a Browning revolver in his pocket. He did so, and tried to make jokes about it."

"What does it mean, in his case," I asked, "'being fatalistic about death'? About death, after all, we all have to be. Had he given up? Did he feel that the problems he was facing were insoluble?"

"Perhaps. Though the evening before his death he decided on a radical change in direction, in a move away from the policy of fulfillment. This would suggest he had by no means given up."

I found this extraordinary. Had he really changed his mind about something so fundamental?

She shrugged.

"Nothing about Walther was simple," she replied. "I remember he once made me read an early essay of his, written in 1904 I think, about weakness and fear. The strong, he'd written, might prevail over the weak, but in the end cleverness prevails over strength. Later he revised his opinion. Of course, like Felix, he was a non-practicing, agnostic Jew. That coloured all his ideas."

What does being non-practicing, agnostic Jew, I wondered, have to do with weakness and fear?

"He thought they were Jewish characteristics. You see, he weighed many of his ideas in terms of their Jewish and non-

Jewish components. Only a few knew this. He was careful about giving his views on Jewish matters to outsiders. For example, he would never say anything publicly against Jews who had come to Germany from Poland and Russia and who did not speak German properly. However much he disliked them. He tried hard not to give the anti-Semites fuel for their fires. But unlike some other Jews in our circle, Walther never denied being a Jew. On the contrary, he proclaimed it and felt a curious sense of responsibility for all German Jews, even though he had formally left the Jewish community. He strongly disagreed with his friend Alfred Kerr—in case you've forgotten, Peter, he's the drama critic of the *Berliner Tageblatt*—whose advice to Jews was to behave as though anti-Semitism didn't exist. Still, I have no doubt Walther hated the Jew within him intensely. He liked muscular blond Prussians."

"The kind who killed him," I said.

"Exactly."

My heart was racing.

"So he was killed by the men he…"

I could not finish the sentence.

"They were Freikorps people. By 1922 as many as 200,000 men belonged to paramilitary units. You know, of course, that the Treaty of Versailles permitted only an army of 100,000, the Reichswehr. There were some who said that Rathenau secretly raised millions to finance the Freikorps."

"He did?" I gasped.

"I did not say he did, Peter. I said there were some who thought he did. I suppose it would have been quite in character at the time. He was afraid of a Bolshevik revolution. He hated chaos. He was a capitalist who favoured a strong state, with large sections of the economy socialized. That's why he even had considerably sympathy for the Bolshevik government in Russia. But of course he didn't want them to take over Germany. There was another factor—the A.E.G. had an interest in doing business in Russia. I told you everything about him was complicated."

I mulled this over for a minute.

"How much did his killers know about him?" I asked.

"A lot, Peter. A lot. They had the greatest respect for him, personally. They killed him for what he represented, the Weimar republic, which they hated, not for what he was. And of course he was a Jew. Which did not prevent them from admiring him as a person. And they wanted that person to be worthy of them, his killers. One of them later wrote about the occasion when they went the adult education building in Frankfurt to hear him speak. I have the book right here. Let me read you the passage:

"'The Minister…was driven by a sense of responsibility and a desire to serve…His magic could work nowhere as well as here. The citizens of this town were proud of the spirit that prevailed within its walls…Rathenau himself had once observed that a statesman should be a mixture of two opposites, he should be half Roman and half Levantine, half good and half devil, like Napoleon and Bismarck…This mixture of two opposing forces was the secret of his own personality. He had the same characteristics as both the great men born in Frankfurt—Goethe and Rothschild.'"[6]

I shook my head in amazement.

"On their list of intended victims," Gertrud went on, "were not only politicians like him, but also bankers such as Max Warburg and Oskar Wassermann, pillars of Weimar finance."

I swallowed hard.

"Was any banker actually attacked?"

"Not as far as I know." That was evidently a question that interested her less than it interested me.

"Were you saying these assassinations have stopped?" I asked her.

"Oh yes. Today's violence is quite different. The murderous days of the Freikorps are over. Today's violence usually takes the form of street battles."

"I suppose that's a step forward," I observed.

"For us, yes. The battles are fought mainly within the working class. With important exceptions on the Right, the middle class has by now, generally speaking, come to terms with the republic. So have the workers who support the social democrats. Nobody loves it, but we accept it. The social democrats, of course, are now part of the governing coalition, a role in which they're far from comfortable. They're used to being in opposition, the way they were in the good old days before 1914. If unemployment continues to get worse, things are bound to change. But on the whole, we've made an amazing recovery. We're much more stable now."

"Have you read *Mein Kampf*?"

"I don't have to. I know all about it, and about the little Bavarian demagogue who wrote it. No, the Nazis don't worry me. What worries me is that there's no successor in sight for Stresemann. You know, Peter, in many ways the turning point for the better was what we've been talking about, Walther's murder. That opened people's eyes. He cared so much for Germany, he would have been deeply moved by the impact his death had on the country. The state funeral, especially the extraordinary speech in the Reichstag the Chancellor Wirth made at his coffin, would have affected him profoundly. Wirth spoke about the monstrous crime that had just been committed against the people of Germany, not merely against the republic. He exclaimed dramatically 'The Enemy stands on the Right!' These words have become famous since. Rathenau would have been immensely gratified by the spontaneous demonstrations against right-wing murderers all over Germany protesting his assassination. The unions declared a general strike for twenty-four hours to honour him, in shame and indignation over his murder. This would have been the occasion for great joy for Walther. It would have been proof that, after all, he had not wasted his life."

7

RED BERLIN

Early in 1929 Peter had become convinced that the forthcoming crash on the New York Stock Exchange was not going to be a temporary glitch but a traumatic downturn, followed by a prolonged, agonizing depression. He promptly decided to make all his own business decisions accordingly.

Now his predictions were beginning to come true. It was the end of October and he was in Berlin. He did not share Ambassador Jacob Gould Schurman's view nor his sister Gertrud's that the worst was over, that the Weimar republic's basic institutions, though unloved, were by now firmly in place. As a matter of fact, the crisis, in a mild form, had already begun during the summer. Unemployment was on the increase. On the Left, the social democrats were the party of the employed, the communists the party of the unemployed.

Peter thought it was only a matter of time before Weimar would crumble. Until he read Bärbl's copy of *Mein Kampf* a little more than three weeks ago, on October 6, he had been sure the dreaded thing would happen, the republic would collapse and the communists would take over, though he knew that there were far more social democrats in Germany than there were communists. To be precise, since the 1928 election there were one hundred fifty-three social democrats in the Reichstag and fifty-four communists. Therefore, he expected the take-over to be violent, as it had been in St. Petersburg twelve years earlier, and to be followed by a civil war.

If only the Left were not so divided! Was there a chance that, once it became clear that they had a common enemy, the two parties could unite against Hitler? When he had sympathized with the social democrats as a boy, he was not yet aware of their internal divisions. Others could see

them, but not he. The social democrats were the opposition to stuffy
autocracy, and that was enough for him. He knew that Berlin was the
centre of socialism, that Karl Marx had been student of Hegel's here, that
it was here that Marx thought through what he had learned, and that it
was here in Berlin that Ferdinand Lasalle, Bismarck's eloquent antagonist,
had formed the first German workers' party. He knew that in Berlin's
municipal parliament in the Kaiser's day the socialists usually received a
majority of votes but had less than a third of the seats, which was due to
the carefully contrived, anti-democratic electoral laws. The situation was
similar elsewhere. Before 1918 the Left was a statistic, not a power.

But after the empire's collapse, in November and December 1918, the
Left became a reality, under the worst possible circumstances. A bloody
civil war broke out on the streets of many German cities, especially Berlin,
largely within the Left. On one side were the provisional president Friedrich
Ebert's social democrats, who, to fight the radicals, had accepted the
assistance of the defeated army's general staff. On the other side were the
'soviets' of the radical workers and farmers. In Munich, the *Räte-
Republik* [Soviet Republic of Bavaria] was improvised, and lasted from
November 1918 to May 1919. The army with the help of right-wing
Freikorps crushed it brutally.

Excerpt from Peter's diary:

<u>Tuesday, October 29th, 1929</u>
I dreamt last night of ambushes, stormtroopers and state funerals.

The plan was that at nine thirty Edwin Rehberg, Uffland's boss at
the *Weltzeitung*, would pick me up and brief me on the politics of the
Left and its views of Hitler, and take me on a tour to the working-class
districts of Wedding and Neukölln. After lunch, after what I expected
to be a depressing morning, I would be compensated by the blissful
beginnings of a *liaison dangereuse* with Brigitte.

While shaving I made two decisions.

One, I would move to a secret hideaway as soon as possible. I'd
think of a suitable place during breakfast. I would not move in with
Gertrud. I would not do that to her. Nor would I check out of the hotel,
which would continue to serve as decoy.

Two, to reduce the risk, I would cut short my stay in Berlin, write
my report to President Hoover on Saturday and leave on Sunday. That

would give me four days of fact-and-opinion-finding, including today. If I stick to the point, that should be enough.

The telephone rang. Two gentlemen were waiting to see me in the lobby. Good. I knew Bernhard Weiss would come through. Hans Bräutigam was round and jolly and Egon Martens tall and thin and had a big, bouncing Adam's apple.

"Have you gentlemen had breakfast?" I asked.

They had. No need to hurry, they said. They would be quite happy waiting for me in the lobby, reading the newspapers.

I myself bought a copy of the *Weltzeitung* and went in the dining-room. As usual, I ordered two boiled eggs in a glass. I can't get that in any hotel or restaurant in the States. I looked at the financial pages. On page three there was a photo of Dr. Horace Greeley Hjalmar Schacht, President of the Reichsbank.

The Finger of God!

At a dinner party in New York two years ago Schacht told me there were three luxury suites reserved for visiting dignitaries on the first floor on the Reichsbank building. (We Americans call it the second floor.) I should not hesitate to make use of this offer, he said, and could always move in at a moment's notice.

The Reichsbank—the perfect hideaway! Why had I not thought of it before? I'm not going to be 100 percent safe anywhere in Berlin. But in the Reichsbank, with proper protection, no doubt about it, I would be 99 percent safe.

Never mind that I can't stand Schacht's sanctimony, his self-right-eousness, his pose of a poet and thinker devoted to things higher than vulgar money, his receding chin, sloping shoulders, that scraggly long neck and the stiff collar that is always too big for him. But what did that have to do with my accepting his gracious hospitality?

How well I remember a dinner party given by the British member of the Committee of Reparations Experts, Sir Charles Addis, in New York three years ago. Schacht once again tried to ingratiate himself with the American bankers, laughing too hard at Jackson Reynold's mildly amus-ing stories about the thirteen children he had fathered. Schacht re-peated several times, with that smug, self-satisfied smile of his, that he was named Hjalmar out of respect for a Danish ancestor, and Horace Greeley because his father, who had spent some time in the United States, had profound admiration for the great journalist and Democratic presidential candidate. After a few drinks he even made up some verses to be sung to the tune of *Yankee Doodle*, to demonstrate his close affinity and deep affection for Americans. He really was intolerable. Yes, I will move to the Reichsbank. Not a single Nazi will find me there.

After breakfast I invited Hans Bräutigam and Egon Martens to my room. I showed them the letter and asked them whether they agreed with me that moving to the Reichsbank would provide a good cover.

They did, very much so, and said they would get in touch with the Reichsbank's security people as soon I had made the arrangements with Schacht's office. I phoned the Reichsbank. One of Schacht's assistants knew who I was and remembered that I had an appointment with his boss the next day. I said I had suddenly decided I needed a change from the Adlon and mentioned the standing invitation. He said, yes, of course, a suite was available. He was sure the Herr President would be delighted that at last I had found it possible to accept his invitation. Unfortunately he was in a meeting. That was quite all right, I said, please do not disturb him, I was seeing him tomorrow anyway and would be able to thank him personally. I would only stay for two or three nights and would arrive by taxi some time in the afternoon.

The best way to come would be through the side entrance on the Kurstrasse, Schacht's assistant said. He would inform the security people at the door.

Now I was ready to meet Edwin Rehberg. On the phone yesterday I had told him, strictly off the record, about my assignment for President Hoover. I said I needed to know more about the Left. Edwin asked me whether I would like to meet the playwright Ernst Toller. I said yes, most emphatically. I had seen one or two of his plays and knew about his role in the *Räte-Republik* of Bavaria. And I also knew of the five-year prison term he received as a result for that role, which enabled him to write his famous expressionist plays.

Edwin was on time. In the car he said Toller was expecting us at a café on the Nettelbeckplatz in Wedding at eleven thirty. I hadn't been in that area since I was fifteen. (I don't go to Harlem either.) He told me about the many courageous public speeches about Nazism, militarism, racism and class justice that Toller had made in the last few years. Toller seemed to me certainly more dangerous to the Nazis than I was, a mere banker on a few days' visit to his home town. And Toller was still alive. So why was I so afraid?

When we were passing the Tempelhof Airport, Edwin related to me the dramatic events that had taken place in Wedding and Neukölln in the first week of May.

"Thirty-three men killed. Some, innocent bystanders. No casualties among the police. Two hundred wounded. Twelve hundred arrested. Civil war, almost."

How did it start?

In April, as the First of May, the traditional workers' holiday, was approaching, I was told that the Berlin police, expecting trouble, no doubt with some reason, prohibited all demonstrations. There had been a great deal of tension lately. Wedding and Neukölln were enemy territory, just as the place had been in the Kaiser's days. The police were acting under orders from their social democratic bosses. This was interpreted by the communists as deliberately provocative. The results were defiance and police violence on a spectacular scale.

By now we had arrived in Neukölln. We were slowly driving along the Hermannstrasse. No wonder one of our American reporters, I forget which one, wrote the other day that Germany was 'the best equipped poorhouse in the world.' the infusion of American capital notwithstanding. Men with hollow cheeks, some with an arm or a leg missing, were standing in doorways, doing nothing. A preview of things to come, I thought. There was a pervasive smell of sour cabbage. Edwin pointed out the spots where they had put up barricades in May.

We drove on.

"Oh, by the way," Edwin said, "we've had quite a response to Uffland's interview with you."

I did not say, 'So did I.' Instead, I asked whether I was wrong to think Hitler will take over a year or two after the coming collapse.

"I think," he said, "that depends largely on Josef Stalin."

"On Josef Stalin?"

"Yes, Peter. On Josef Stalin. Last year, he ordered communist parties everywhere not to cooperate on any level with social democrats in the class struggle against the 'capitalist bourgeoisie.' He calls them 'social fascists.' Before that, in Germany, the two parties on the Left had occasionally voted together on a number of issues. But no longer. Now, suppose you're right and the Nazis will do well once the economy goes really wrong, Stalin may very well order the German communists to back them to crush the common enemy, the social democrats."

"My dear Edwin," I exclaimed. "Obviously Stalin has not read *Mein Kampf*. For Hitler he's the archenemy. He makes that very clear."

"My dear Peter, I'm sure he knows all about *Mein Kampf*. That won't bother him in the least. He's an orthodox Marxist. He prides himself on taking the long view. He'll consider the Nazis the last phase of imperialist capitalism. He thinks once Hitler has been in power for a while, his, Stalin's, communists will easily toss him aside and proclaim the Dictatorship of the Proletariat."

"What a dreadful, dreadful delusion!" I was getting excited. "Is that what the German communists think, too?"

"Ask Paul Levi when you see him. He'll know. No doubt some of them do, when they have time to think about such things. At the moment they're being kept busy fighting on two fronts, against the social democrats on one, and against the Nazis on the other. To the communists here, the social democrats are by far greater menace. In early May, six months ago, the Nazis stood aside, thoroughly enjoying the spectacle of their two enemies fighting it out."

Notes

Ernst Toller, thirty-five, wearing shirt sleeves and a worker's cap, chain-smoking, intense, with dark eyes and wavy hair, was waiting for us at his favourite café on the Nettelbeckplatz in Wedding, corner Reinickendorfer Strasse, at the border of the area that had been blocked off during the emergency in May.

"Ernst, the time has come at last," Edwin began, "that you will write a play about an American banker from Berlin who's read *Mein Kampf* and was transformed. He thinks the author of that great work will become Germany's redeemer. The banker's name is Peter Hammersmith. Here he is."

"How delightful." Toller's style was Kurfürstendamm, not Wedding. "I didn't know the book had crossed the Atlantic."

"As far as I know," I said, "only one copy has. Mine."

"Did you actually read it?"

"Enough to get the general idea."

Toller looked at me and smiled.

"I don't think I can write a play about a nice man who is also a banker. I learned many years ago a serious writer must never, ever allow reality to upset his preconceptions. For me, you see, bankers are class enemies."

"Well then," Edwin laughed, "let Peter write a book about you. He does not suffer from any preconceptions. He's totally objective. You're a great subject. In 1914, a twenty-one year-old middle-class idealist from somewhere east of Berlin by the name of Ernst Toller enthusiastically welcomes the war and happily joins the army. The last thing he expects is death in the trenches, under very disagreeable conditions. He becomes a pacifist and a socialist. Five years after 1914, in 1919, he finds himself, to his extreme surprise, at the centre of a violent revolution in Munich, run by two saintly intellectuals, one a brilliant journalist, the other a great Shakespeare scholar. Soon, both are murdered. The young man survives and is sent to prison. There, once again to his great surprise, he writes a number of extraordinary plays, which were translated into twenty-seven languages and performed all over the civilized world while he was still safely behind bars."

"Yes," I declared, "obviously that would be a splendid subject for me. If I were a writer instead of a banker. And not, I must insist, a socialist banker. By the way, you and Adolf Hitler were both in prison in Bavaria, more or less at the same time. Did you ever meet him?"

"No. I was first. He came later. But one of my fellow prisoners met him early in 1919 in a Munich barracks. He still called himself a social democrat at the time. My informant took an instant dislike to him. Hitler was conceited and puffed up, he said, like a man who's read many books and digested none."

"Wrong," Edwin observed. "He'd read only a few books, the wrong ones, and digested them only too well."

"Maybe. But the interesting thing my friend told me was something else. Hitler was in the hospital, suffering from shellshock, blind, while the war came to an end, the Kaiser abdicated and the republic was proclaimed. When he recovered his sight, the world had changed. That made me think. A man who can go blind in the face of things he does not wish to see, I thought, must possess extraordinary strength of mind. At that moment I decided to take Hitler seriously."

"Have you written about him?"

"In a curious way, I have. Without intending to. Early in 1923 I wrote a comedy called *Der Entfesselte Wotan* [Wotan Unbound]. That was before Hitler's attempted his putsch in November, which made all the headlines. Very few people had heard of him. My hero was a megalomaniac barber, a latherer, a demagogue who was disillusioned by postwar Germany and started a colony in Brazil. I got the idea from a fellow prisoner. I wasn't thinking of Hitler at all. My Wotan was a crazy nationalist and anti-Semite. I was making fun of Wagner's Wotan, obviously. There were all kinds of strange parallels with the early Hitler, including an absurdly lenient prison sentence. But that was purely accidental. I made it all up. All this irrational craziness, all this lather, was in the air. Hitler just came along and embodied it. Critics said I had read *Mein Kampf*. But he didn't dictate the book until 1924 and it wasn't published until the fall of 1925. I wrote my play in 1923."

"However, " Edwin interrupted him, "when they performed *Wotan Unbound* here in Berlin in 1926 you didn't object when they made the resemblance to Hitler explicit."

"Yes, that's absolutely true. As a matter of fact, I jumped at the chance. It was a great opportunity. I wanted to warn the world against Hitler. But before that, in the first two productions, in Moscow and in Prague, my barber was just a barber. For the Berlin production I also changed the ending."

"Why did you do that?"

"Because in 1926 I suddenly decided the Nazis were a serious threat, and not a bunch of bunglers. They had given up putschism. They decided to come to power legally. You're absolutely right, Herr Hammersmith. The world had better pay attention. They have the leadership, energy, shrewdness, organization and, above all, hunger for power all the others lack."

"And you say so publicly?"

"I certainly do. But nobody listens. Some think, if they come to power, it can't last long, after all, none of our governments do. These yokels are not equipped to govern. People don't see the obvious. If it happens, theirs won't be a mild, transitional kind of Fascism. They will be ruthless, diabolical. They will destroy everything that's worthwhile. And who will be to blame? We will be to blame, we who in 1919 had no confidence in the people, no confidence in ourselves, we who botched the revolution, who allowed our best people to be murdered, who were too young, too immature, too utopian, too disunited to do what we were supposed to do. We did not understand the mentality of our opponents, the bourgeoisie. We did not grasp that they had been thoroughly demoralized by the war and the way it ended, and that they were reluctant to give up any of the little power they still had. We did not understand that, for their own reasons, they were thoroughly opposed to any changes whatsoever, and that the last thing they wanted was to listen to the wishes of the vast majority of ordinary people who wanted to bring about fundamental reforms."

"Ernst, I think you're too hard on yourself," Edwin said. "Most of your difficulties you inherited."

"Some, perhaps. The backbone of the older generation of socialists was broken in 1914, when they backed the war and hated themselves for it ever since. They would have been the experienced leaders we so desperately needed in 1918. And of course, people like myself found it impossible to work in harmony with dogmatic communists who followed orders that came from far away and had nothing to do with our needs."

These were not matters on which I could speak. I looked at my watch. We were already late. I did not wish to keep Brigitte waiting. But I couldn't leave on this note of gloom.

"Who can now stand in Hitler's way?" I asked.

"I see only one chance. I expect nothing from the political parties. Only the free trade unions have the power to block the Nazis. But they must act together. Which is the difficulty. Seven million workers have a lot of clout. I'm concentrating all my attention on them."

I wished him luck.

The Record

Towards the end of February 1933, Toller left Berlin for Switzerland where he was to make a series of radio broadcasts. Two hours after the outbreak of the Reichstag fire on February 27, S.A. stormtroopers broke into his flat to arrest him. Not finding him, they ransacked his belongings and subsequently destroyed his papers. He never returned to Germany.

In the six years that were left of his life he was one of the most prominent representatives of 'The Other Germany,' in England and in the United States. In 1935, the Irish playwright Sean O'Casey wrote: 'England will be striding nearer to a finer drama when Toller has his London season.' But Toller never had his London season, and his plays were only performed in theatre clubs and by socialist drama groups.

When civil war broke out in Spain, he soon recognized it as a dress rehearsal for the war he saw coming. He went to Barcelona to see for himself what was happening. He pleaded with the western democracies to change their policy of non-intervention. He helped organize food relief for the Spanish people, with he support, among others, of Mrs. Eleanor Roosevelt. He saw the defeat of the republican side as another revolution betrayed.

On May 19, 1939, General Francisco Franco held a victory parade in Madrid. Three days later, in a New York hotel room, Ernst Toller hanged himself.

8

PETER IN LOVE

Peter first met Charlie Chaplin in the Alexandria Hotel in Los Angeles, during a trip to the West Coast in 1919, to take part in financial discussions that later led to the formation of United Artists, the independent distribution company in which Charlie, Douglas Fairbanks Jr., Mary Pickford and W. S. Hart were to be principals.

In 1923, Peter read about Hitler in Germany, when the papers reported the news of the abortive beer hall putsch in Munich. He did not see his photograph. The first time he saw one was during a visit to Berlin in June 1925. He was immediately struck by the striking resemblance with Charlie Chaplin. But at the time Hitler was only a marginal figure. There was no reason for Peter to ponder the significance.

He met Charlie again two years later, in August 1925 in New York, during the New York premiere of *The Gold Rush* in the Strand Theatre. On two or three occasions, while he was watching the film, the curious resemblance with that Bavarian adventurer flashed through his mind. He had not bothered to remember his name, and soon forgot about it. It was far more important that Charlie introduced him to the enchanting Louise Brooks with whom he was having an affair. She was nineteen, half Charlie's age.

Born in Cherryvale, Kansas, Louise had been a dancer on Broadway in the Ziegfeld's Follies. In the same year she made her film debut in Hollywood, where she played two leading roles. Soon after, she attracted the attention of the German film director G. W. Pabst, who invited her to Berlin to play Lulu. That is when she made film history. In 1930, she returned to the United States. After a few years she could not abide Hollywood any longer and abandoned the cinema for good to live in seclusion in Rochester, New York, until she died in 1985. In 1982 she published a series of autobiographical essays, *Lulu in Hollywood*.

In 1979, the English theatre critic Kenneth Tynan re-discovered her.

> She has run through my life like a magnetic thread—this shameless urchin tomboy, this unbroken, unbreakable porcelain filly. She is a prairie princess, equally at home in a waterfront bar and in the royal suite at Neuschwanstein; a creature of impulse, a temptress with no pretensions, capable of dissolving into a giggling fit at a peak of erotic ecstasy; amoral but totally selfless, with that sleek jet *cloche* of hair that rings such a peal of bells in my subconscious...[7]

In her interview with Tynan Louise described her affair with Charlie Chaplin with whom she had lived 'for two happy months' in 1935.

> Ever since he died [in 1977], my mind has gone back fifty years. trying to define that lovely being from another world. He not only created The Little Fellow, though that was miracle enough. He was a self-made aristocrat. He taught himself to speak cultivated English, and he kept a dictionary in the bathroom at his hotel so that he could learn a new word every morning. While he dressed, he prepared his script for the day, which was intended to adorn his private portrait of himself as a perfect English gentleman. He was also a sophisticated lover, who had affairs with Peggy Hopkins Joyce and Marion Davies and Pola Negri, and he was a brilliant businessman, who owned his films and demanded fifty percent of the gross—which drove Nick Schenck wild, along with all the other people who were plotting to rob him. Do you know, I can't once remember him *still?* He was always standing up as he sat down, and going out as he came in. Except when he turned off the lights and went to sleep. without liquor of pills, like a child...And how he paid

attention! We were hypnotized by the beauty
and inexhaustible originality of this glistening
creature.[8]

Excerpt from Peter's diary:

<u>Tuesday, October 29th, 1929</u>

One of the themes in the world's greatest literature is the conflict
between Desire and Principle.

Brigitte was waiting for me in the Adlon lobby where we were to
meet. The head bobbed, the skin white as milk, the neck graceful as a
swan's. She'd taken off her coat. Her dress was pale blue, the skirt short.
Whether Principle (is that another word for Caution?) would prevail
over Desire would largely depend on our conversation. My two police
protectors, the puffy-cheeked Hans Bräutigam and the tall, skinny Egon
Martens were sitting a few chairs away. They really were perfect. They
looked like prosperous businessmen. Of course they could not know
that the stunning girl whom they were eyeing was waiting for me. I
gave them a non-committal smile when I came in.

Brigitte and I went into the dining room. The two policemen followed, but sat down out of earshot. After studying the menu Brigitte
ordered eel with dill sauce, and I Königsberger Klopse, meat balls with
capers and sardellen sauce, to be washed down with a light Mosel.

Notes

"Tell me something about Josef von Sternberg," I said as
the waiter poured the wine.

"Everybody here loves him. Everybody except me. When
he arrived in August he gave a press conference and said, 'I
feel as if I died in Hollywood and have now awakened in
heaven.' And he hadn't even met his new star yet. Dietrich
can't wait to go to bed with him. Did you know that she's
been married for six years? They even have a little girl! She
was twenty-one when she married. Rudi is an assistant director."

"Do you know him?"

"No, I only know the gossip. I love gossip. I also love being gossiped about. I hope there'll be lots of gossip about you and me."

"So do I. Did you see *Pandora's Box?*"

"No, I'm sorry I missed it."

"I only mention it because the girl who plays the lead looks exactly like you."

"So someone told me." She tried to think of the name. "She's an American, isn't she?"

"Yes, Louise Brooks. She played Lulu. A destroyer of men. Every man she has sex with dies."

"Oh, now I remember." She nearly shouted. "Von Sternberg talked about her. It's because of Lulu that his Dietrich character is called Lola.[9] That wasn't at all her name in the original novel. There she was only *Die Künstlerin Fröhlich* [the artist Fröhlich]. No first name. Lola destroys Emil Jannings. And in some magazine I read an article about the man who wrote the play on which the film is based."

"Frank Wedekind."

"Oh yes, that was the name. He believed in free love, and not in obeying the rules. Now it all comes back to me. Marlene Dietrich wanted to play Lulu for Pabst. But Pabst chose Louise Brooks. He thought Dietrich lacked the innocence and freshness he was looking for. I don't blame him. He thought Brooks was perfect. Do you know her?"

"When Charlie Chaplin had an affair with her, in 1925," I replied, "he introduced her to me."

"Oh!" She clapped her hands in delight. "I nearly forgot! You're a friend of Charlie Chaplin!"

I nodded.

"And did you ever see her again afterwards, just the two of you?"

"As a matter of fact, I did. I once had a drink with her, in the Plaza Hotel. That's all."

"Why didn't you invite her to dinner?"

"I did, but she made it clear I wasn't her type."

"How ridiculous! And Charlie was her type?"

"Obviously."

"Did she talk about him?"

"About nothing else. She said he was a most generous lover."

"Like you," she said, stroking my hand.

"Are you seducing me?" I asked.

"Yes! Let's go to your room! Fast!"

"Not until we've had our dessert."

I was amazed I was, against all my own expectations, a Man of Principle. At least for the moment.

"Have you read *Mein Kampf*?" I asked.

"What a question!" she exclaimed, dumbfounded. "At a time like this. Are you testing me?"

"Yes."

"No, I've not read it. But I can tell you a lot about the Nazis. Somebody showed me your interview on Monday in the *Berliner Weltzeitung*. I don't agree with you at all. I think Adolf Hitler is right about a lot of things. Do I get good marks for being honest with you? After all, I could easily have said, I agree with every word you said. So let's forget about the dessert and go upstairs. Right now. Hurry, hurry!"

No more Principle. No more Caution.

Excerpt from Peter's diary:

<u>Tuesday, October 29th, 1929</u>

We made love in my room until, alas, she had to go to Neubabelsberg to a rehearsal. We were to meet again for lunch tomorrow, at Kempinsky's. After she left I took a cab to see my old friend Alphonse Friedberg on the Kurfürstendamm, jeweller to the House of Hohenzollern and many others who, even if they lost their thrones, have not lost their bank accounts and can easily afford to help maintain Alphonse's very agreeable pre-war standard of living.

Alphonse looks as though he might very well be Albert Einstein's younger brother. He has the same melancholy expression, the same worldly-wise, sad eyes. (I don't know whether Einstein has a little brother. I may ask him on Friday morning when I see him.) Unlike the rumpled Albert, Alphonse is always impeccably dressed and usually wears a pink pearl on his blue silk tie.

I asked Alphonse whether he had anything on the Charlie Chaplin theme. Nobody knows more about marital and extramarital love than an imaginative, first-class jeweller. The profession demands that jewellers be experts in the ways that gentlemen woo and reward ladies. Since he knows me and knows that I am a friend of Charlie Chaplin, he understood immediately that I wanted to reward a lady who was amused by my knowing him. There was no need to waste valuable time dwelling on the obvious. All I had to say was that I needed it by lunch-time tomorrow. Alphonse merely nodded solemnly and went to the back of the store. After about five minutes he emerged with a brooch he had improvised at his worktable. I knew he was a great artist, but I had hardly dared to expect a composition as perfect as this. The head was a diamond face with a ruby moustache, topped by an onyx hat. The body consisted of emeralds and sapphires, with amethysts as boots. The cane was an ordinary wooden matchstick. All he needed, Alphonse said, was a couple of hours for his technicians to 'glue the thing together.' It would be ready in time. I could pick it up before lunch tomorrow.

• • •

The Reichsbank was a sumptuous Renaissance palazzo three blocks south of Unter den Linden, facing the Jägerstrasse. The private suites were on the second floor, close to the board room and the presidential quarters. All windows had iron gates.

When Peter's taxi dropped him at the side entrance at the Oberwallstrasse at six fifteen, he was looking forward to half an hour of rest before setting out to have dinner with the Lindhoffs.

He had told Hans Bräutigam and Egon Martens he was going to be at the Reichsbank at six, or soon thereafter. They were waiting for him.

"We'd like to tell you something you should know," Bräutigam said solemnly as Peter descended from the taxi. "Do you think we could come in with you for a minute?"

"Of course." Peter's heart pounded as he pressed the doorbell.

A uniformed, gold-braided valet opened the door. "Herr Hammersmith?" He looked as though he had served as a staff officer under

General Ludendorff at army headquarters. He had been informed, he said, that police headquarters had requested space for Peter's two security guards, so presumably that's who Peter's companions were. They instinctively clicked their heels. The valet took the three of them to the second floor, on a very slow, pre-war elevator. It would have been faster to walk up.

Peter's suite was twice the size of the room he had at the Adlon. A vase of pink carnations stood on a Louis XVI desk. The valet withdrew respectfully.

They sat down in a corner, near the window.

"We think you should know that among the young lady's many friends is a stormtrooper by the name of Horst Zahlendorf. He is a bartender at the Hotel Siegfried in Lichterfelde."

What a relief!

"I see." Peter pretended to be hugely upset. "Good work. Thank you."

Peter did not wish to confess that his previous knowledge of the stormtrooper's existence had not stood in the way of the young lady becoming his young lady. Even if not only his.

"Our people have a file on him," Bräutigam added. "We're having him watched."

"Thank you. I think that's a very sound precaution. Gentlemen, I now need some rest."

9

MARGARETE

Peter Hammersmith did not go to New York in 1904 to escape the stuffy autocracy of the Kaiser's Germany. He came to follow Margarete Schulenberg, a practitioner of free love, who had been playing the femme fatale Lulu in an amateur production of Frank Wedekind's *Earth Spirit*. That was also the year in which the young late romantic Viennese composer Alban Berg met the older Arnold Schönberg who changed his life, an event that led directly to the twelve-tone composition of the opera *Lulu*. It was based on the same material and had its première in Zürich in 1937. Berg died in 1935. He might have been amused to learn that even a contemporary Wall Street millionaire could be preoccupied with Wedekind's ideas on the connection between love, sex and death.

Margarete returned to Berlin. She and Peter remained good friends. Just before the war she married Peter's classmate at the Fichte Gymnasium, the young doctor Teddy Lindhoff. Both Teddy's parents had been friends of the Hammerschmidt family. His father had been their pediatrician. The Lindhoffs lived in a high-ceilinged apartment on the Emserstrasse in Wilmersdorf, a block away from the Hammerschmidts' apartment in the Pommersche Strasse. Peter came over from America for the wedding.

Fifteen years later Margarete no longer believed in free love. She was now in her early forties and was still as attractive as ever. The Lindhoffs had a splendid marriage, and two boys. Peter was sure Margarete never told Teddy about their pre-marital affair.

Since Peter's visit to Berlin in 1920, after his parents had died, he had been back several times and visited the Lindhoffs in their apartment. During the war Teddy had been a medical officer, always just behind the lines.

The experience had had a traumatic impact. After the war he went back to medical school and became a psychiatrist. At the same time he became intensely interested in politics and began to make frequent contributions to conservative, anti-Weimar publications. He had never written anything before, other than medical and psychiatric papers. This interest was entirely new, the consequence of the war and the way it ended.

Teddy wrote to Peter about his articles but never offered to send them to him. Peter never asked for them. Nor did they ever talk about them on Peter's visits.

Excerpt from Peter's diary:

Tuesday, October 29th, 1929

While the maid was serving the soup Teddy reminded me of a letter he had written to me after my first successes on Wall Street. He wasn't at all astonished, he had written, 'you always had a sixth sense.' Did I remember that?

Yes, I did. I'd taken it as a compliment, I said. I also remember my answer. I didn't have a sixth sense at all, I said. I was governed by nothing other than Pure Reason.

"A man after my own heart," Margarete remarked.

I told them about my entirely reasonable response to *Mein Kampf* and my mission for President Hoover.

"You could not be more wrong, Peter," Teddy remarked. "On every count."

"Except one," Margarete said. "You're right that Hitler is an unsavoury, thoroughly unappetizing character."

"Oh yes," Teddy agreed. "Of course. But that's not important. As a matter of fact, even though—I repeat, even though—I don't think he's important at all politically, not in the least, I've taken a professional interest in the case. After reading the man's book. And after talking to a few people about him who know him."

"You have? Tell me."

"I'm particularly curious about a few things. For example, his alleged hypnotic powers."

"I hear he's a mesmerizing orator," I said.

"So they say," Margarete said. "I understand he's developed quite a technique."

"I've been studying the diverse psychic effect we all have on others," Teddy resumed. "Every one of us in a different way. Hypnotism is just one way of affecting others—intentionally. But of course we also have involuntary effects on others. Some of us are *sympathique*. Others are *antipathique*. Each of us transmits on a different wavelength. And each of us has a different receiving mechanism. There are explanations for all these things. Receivers have models in their minds that give rise to expectations. That's the sort of thing I'm looking at."

"I think Hitler has learned to play Svengali," Margarete declared. "There's nothing involuntary about it at all. He probably practices in front of a mirror."

Teddy smiled. "I think you well may be right. There's a lot of talk about the way he looks deeply into your eyes when he shakes your hand. It's supposed to be unforgettable, that stare. I understand some people in his crowd make of fun of him behind his back."

"They won't," I said gravely, "once he's in power."

"That will never happen. Never."

"Ernst Toller told me this morning about Hitler's shellshock in November 1918. Apparently he was in the hospital, blind. Toller said a man who could go blind in the face of things he did not wish to see had to be taken seriously. He had to have extraordinary will power. What do you think of that, Teddy?"

"Hitler is quite specific about this in *Mein Kampf*. As you may remember, Peter. His account differs considerably from that of Toller's. Of course in his book he tries to create his own myth, but for once he may be telling the truth. He says that on October 13, 1918, the English used yellow-cross gas, in their attack at Ypres. He was there and his eyes turned into glowing coals. Everything grew dark around him, he wrote. He was sent to the army hospital in Pasewalk, east of Berlin, in Pomerania. There, he says, he experienced—I'm quoting from memory—'the greatest villainy in history'."

"The German surrender," Margarete said.

"Exactly. Those are not the words he uses. He uses the words 'high treason.' He says he wept when he heard the news, the first time since he had stood at his mother's grave. He talks about the terrible days and nights that followed. He never spells out that the German army had not been beaten, that therefore no one had the right to sue for an armistice, nor to mutiny, as the sailors did in Kiel. That is understood. What he does say is that before the disaster Kaiser Wilhelm had been the first German emperor to hold out a conciliatory hand to the leaders of Marxism, without suspecting that the scoundrels have no honour. Incidentally, to Hitler, Marxists and Jews are the same. While they, the Marxists, still held the imperial hand in theirs, the other hand was reaching for the dagger."

"I suppose," I said, trying to grasp what Teddy was saying, "that when he referred to the conciliatory hand he meant the concessions to the opposition the Kaiser made at the last minute in favour of parliamentary   reforms?"

"Presumably," Teddy agreed. "But the important thing is a passage that followed. I remember it exactly: 'There is no making pacts with Jews,' he wrote. 'There can only be the hard "either/or." I, for my part, have decided to go into politics'."

"What's he saying?" Margarete asked. "He went into politics to take revenge on the Jews?"

"Something like that, I suppose. He did not tell us what form the revenge was to take. The amazing thing I've discovered, by talking to a man who knew him in Vienna before the war, is that his opinions on the Jews at that time were, let us say, ambiguous. Hitler maintained that Jews were members of a different race and had a different smell, but at the same time he admired the way Jews managed to survive their persecution and he had some Jewish friends. He praised the eighteenth-century Austrian jurist Joseph von Sonnenfels, a converted Jew who opposed the death penalty and edited a magazine called *The Man without Prejudice*. When someone complained that there were not enough monuments to honour the Jewish poet Heinrich Heine, Hitler quite agreed and said that, while he did not like Heine's views, he respected his poetry. And when it was said that Jews could not be artists Hitler disagreed and pointed to Mendelssohn and Offenbach. He discussed religious questions and the future of Zionism with Jews. And he preferred to sell his watercolour paintings to Jewish dealers, because he thought they were more honest and gave him better prices."

"You didn't read any of that in *Mein Kampf*," Margarete observed.

"Certainly not. There he goes to great lengths to describe how he hated Jews from the moment he first saw them. But that was written, or rather dictated, more than five years after whatever it was that happened to his psyche in November 1918. He may well have had some sort of hallucinatory episode in that hospital. It may have had a profound effect on him. By 1924 he was myth-making."

"May I change the subject slightly?" Margarete asked. "Tell me this, Peter. Am I dreaming or is it true that you know Charlie Chaplin?"

"Oh yes," I said. "We've been friends for years and see each other occasionally. Why do you ask?"

"Because Adolf Hitler always reminds me of him. I can never take him seriously because I always think he's playing Charlie Chaplin."

Teddy and I laughed.

"You see," Margaret continued without joining in the laughter, "the two of them have a lot in common. Did you know they were born within a few days of each other? Chaplin was born on April 16th, 1889, and Hitler on April 20th. I'm not superstitious about this sort of thing, and of course this means nothing in itself." She paused for a moment, frowning. 'The question is," she said, "since I'm not superstitious, why do I mention it?"

"Because coincidences make us uncomfortable," Teddy said.

"Maybe." Margarete shrugged. "In his early days in the men's flophouses Hitler must have met many tramps like Charlie Chaplin."

"What an interesting idea!" Teddy exclaimed. "For both, their early memories of misery among the outcasts of society must have been decisive. These memories must have become an important source of their anger. They just worked it out differently. What a contrast! Charlie Chaplin is an absolutely serious person, a great artist. He's obviously one of those rare geniuses who's caught the spirit of the times exactly, instinctively."

"And Adolf Hitler?" Margaret asked.

"He's a buffoon," Teddy replied. "Totally out of tune with the Zeitgeist."

Notes

"Adolf Hitler," Teddy declared, "is a passing phenomenon, not to be taken seriously. You can reassure your president, Peter. And yourself. He's unworthy of the movement he's exploiting."

"But the movement is important?" I asked.

"It could not be more important. It was born in the war and is carried by a generation that understands that the only measure of life's values is—please forgive me, Peter, for striking this note—their relationship to death."

"For once," Margarete observed, "Peter is tongue-tied."

"I don't blame him," Teddy smiled. "This is a far cry from his Democrats and Republicans. The war has done things to us it has not done to other people."

"The French and British have also lost a generation of young men on the battlefield," I said. "What's the difference?"

"In 1914 France and England were already nations," Teddy replied. "But here in Germany, we had no nation yet. We had a people. The people went to war in 1914, and in 1918 came home a nation, a community of citizens. Before the war it had never occurred to anybody that ordinary people, even women, had an obligation to do voluntary work for strangers. This was unheard of in peacetime. Nobody had any sense of civic duty. One obeyed orders, that was all. As you know, Peter, Germany is retarded. It was not until the war that German national feeling in a modern, contemporary sense was born. Before, our nationalism was a combination of poetic and musical nostalgia and Prussian militarism, culminating in a caricature of a Kaiser from the ancient House of Hohenzollern who had an inferiority complex, especially in relation to his ancestor Frederick the Great. He was trying to compete with his fellow imperialists who usually were more grown up and bet-

ter at the game than he was. I've never blamed you for running away from that circus, Peter."

"That's not why he left at all," Margarete volunteered.

I tried to kick her under the table but missed.

"Peter left because he was looking for the ideal woman,"
she said.

"Is that right, Peter?" Teddy smiled.

"Absolutely."

"I understand you found one," Teddy said.

"Yes," I replied, feeling like a complete fool. "Catherine
and I have an excellent marriage."

"You certainly didn't have to leave because of the Kaiser.
You knew perfectly well that in his day civilized people could
lead a perfectly civilized life, without any interference. Unless
they wanted to upset the system, which you certainly didn't.
And people could make a lot of money, if that's what they
wanted to do. The point I'm trying to make is that modern
German nationalism was created in the war. I'm a psychiatrist, Peter. I know what the war did to men's minds. No one
who's been through it is the same as he was before it. Very few
can talk about it. You'll say the French and the British, and
even the Americans, also went through it, and look at them.
To which I'll answer that most men, but by no means all, were
damaged by the war in some way, whatever the nationality.
There are some German thinkers—Ernst Jünger is one of
them—who believe that the best of our men were spiritually
enriched by the war. I understand that, and even admire it in
some way. But only Germans were betrayed and humiliated
by the way the war ended. And blamed for having caused it."

"Ernst Toller," I said, "was turned into a pacifist and into
an ardent advocate of social justice."

"That, of course, is one perfectly honourable response, even
if I consider it misguided," Teddy replied. "It isn't my response,
nor the response of the people I admire most. We don't think
the main issue is non-violence versus violence, nor social justice in Toller's sense. Pacifism, in my view, is based on wishful
thinking and takes a superficial, far too optimistic view of
human nature. It assumes that most men are adequately
equipped with the old-fashioned virtues we cherish most, virtues like honour, decency, courage, comradeship, loyalty, hero-

ism, sacrifice and obedience. But they're not, clearly. We think that new book everybody's talking about, *All's Quiet on the Western Front,* is one-sided and shallow. We believe in a new organic, harmonious, orderly, mutually respectful society in which everyone recognizes that it's absurd to believe we're all equal. Anyone who has eyes knows that is not true. The fiction of human equality leads directly to rule by inferior, cynical mediocrities, where more stress is laid on intellectual and material rather than on spiritual values, where the lowest common denominator invariably prevails. We want to undo the seamy side of the French Revolution and return to a truly democratic, tolerant Christian society run by an educated and morally sensitive and responsible elite."

"So much for Adolf Hitler," Margaret observed.

"Exactly," her husband agreed. "And we reject the idea of a biological basis of nationhood."

"You used the word 'democratic', Teddy," I said. "It's of course evident that Nature did not make us all equal. But the idea of equality that came out of the French Revolution was political. How can you have a democracy without political equality?"

"You can. You must. In our view, democracy means the will of the people. The *volonté générale.* Jean-Jacques Rousseau. Him, we like. No constitution, no parliament, no political party must be allowed to obstruct the will of the people. The democracy we want to establish is not liberal. We oppose individualism. Weimar is foreign to us. It's alien, un-German. We don't believe in mechanical vote-counting. We look at Weimar as a degenerate bourgeois system. We don't accept it and we don't play according to its rules."

By now we were enjoying the main course, a roast of lamb. The red wine was excellent.

"And who exactly is 'we'?"

"'We' are the upholders of the idea of a conservative revolution. We've worked out our ideas since 1919, in universities and in youth groups, among kindred spirits in the professions, more or less in private, without seeking public approval, and therefore without attracting the scorn of Weimar intellectuals."

Teddy elaborated his ideas until we had finished the dessert. I did not want to tell him what seemed obvious to me, that his conservative revolutionaries were unwittingly paving the way for Adolf Hitler who would sweep them aside when the time came.

"What do you think would happen," I asked him at last, "if there's an economic crisis with large-scale unemployment and misery? Whom would you prefer to take over, the communists or the Nazis?"

"Obviously I would prefer the Nazis. Because I have no doubt that by then they would have disposed of Hitler. There are too many sensible people on the Right who understand that a vulgar version of Charlie Chaplin has no role to play in the New Germany."

The Record

Teddy Lindhoff is an invented character. The model for him was Edgar Jung, lawyer and political scientist, the author of Die Herrschaft der Minderwertigen, ihr Zerfall und ihre Ablösung *[The Rule of the Inferior, Their Disintegration and Succession].*[10]

Jung became adviser to Franz von Papen who became chancellor in 1932 and Hitler's vice-chancellor in 1933. He fought the Nazis fearlessly before and after they came to power and was widely thought to have had a hand in writing von Papen's Marburg speech of June 17, 1934, which was severely critical of Hitler.

On June 25, 1934, Jung was arrested. During The Night of the Long Knives of June 30th, 1934—the 'Röhm Putsch'—he was shot to death. Von Papen was put under house arrest. He subsequently accepted the posts of Minister in Vienna and Ambassador to Turkey. In 1946 at Nuremberg he was indicted as a war criminal. He was acquitted.

10

THE PHONY PRINCE

One sleeps very well in the Reichsbank, Peter observed when he woke up on Wednesday morning. He felt fine. Needing time to himself to make notes on yesterday's conversations, he wanted to keep the morning free. In the afternoon, after lunch with Brigitte who had a rehearsal at three, he was to see Hjalmar Schacht, not a pleasant prospect, and spend the evening with his old friend Bernhard Weiss, the vice-president of the Berlin Police, who was an intense character and usually not very humorous. It was likely to be a strenuous evening.

His suite was equipped with a radio. Half absent-mindedly he turned it on. What he heard was fascinating. It was a replay of a talk by a man called Harry Domela who, three years earlier, had successfully impersonated Prince Wilhelm of Prussia for many weeks. The prince was the eldest son of the Crown Prince and therefore the successor to the non-existent imperial throne. Domela was caught and put in prison, where he wrote a bestseller about his experiences, evidently more amusing than the other book written in prison not so long ago that Peter had in part financed. Domela had had some legal troubles because the cover showed a picture of the real Prince Wilhelm.

Curiously, Peter had never heard of Domela. The talk was recorded on a disc in a prison in Cologne around the time the book was published. It was not clear why it was repeated today. The editors are grateful for the Berlin Radio Station in Königswusterhausen, which kindly made the text of the talk available. What follows is an abridged version.

• • •

Harry Domela Tells His Story[12]

I have no use for the Kaiser, nor his family. Nor do I look like Prince Wilhelm. To judge from his photographs, he's well built and strong. I am not.

I understood very well I could not get away with playing the prince for long and was quite familiar with jail. I knew you always get enough to eat there, which was a distinct advantage over not being in jail. So I was reconciled to ending up with another prison term when the curtain came down, as it was bound to. More than reconciled, in fact. Actually, quite pleased because this time, by pure accident, I managed to perform an important public service. Good fortune, sheer chance, had given me the opportunity to demonstrate to a wide public that large numbers of citizens at the symbolic centre of the republic, citizens in the immediate vicinity of Weimar itself, remain profoundly, unswervingly loyal to the House of Hohenzollern. Which means that they pretend that there has never been a revolution and, by implication, that Germany has not lost the war.

May I repeat, I did not wake up one morning and decide 'Today I will pretend to be Prince Wilhelm, to teach Germans a lesson in good republican citizenship.' It was purely a matter of luck. It would never have occurred to me to play Prince Wilhelm if people had not wanted me to be Prince Wilhelm. Who am I to resist the will of the people?

I come from Latvia. But I'm German, even though I still don't have German nationality. My father died when I was four. My family did not belong to the nobility, and we were not rich, but in the old Kurland, where I come from, we Baltic Germans were always on top and behaved accordingly, even though it was Russia, not Germany. I've often been told that I was a natural aristocrat. This is simply because I'm well brought up and was taught good manners. Before the opportunity arose for me to become a phony prince, I had to spend many years being a phony proletarian and living like a dog.

In 1914, I was eleven when the German army moved into Kurland. I was separated from my mother and sent to a municipal establishment for eighty refugee children in Riga, run by a Russian. There we were starved and beaten, for four years. In 1918, the Russian Bolsheviks helped the Latvians take revenge on us Germans for centuries of oppression. In the spring of 1919, the Freikorps came in to fight the Bolsheviks. I joined them and ended up in the Baltic Landeswehr. I wasn't fifteen yet. I was in heaven, free at last. The perfect education for a teenager.

I witnessed the most horrible scenes imaginable. We fought everybody, the Bolsheviks, the Latvians, the Lithuanians. I loved every minute of it. But, for having fought the Latvians I was promptly expelled from the newly formed Latvian republic. In January 1920, I was told my mother had been killed. Not much later I found myself in the most desolate part of the Mark Brandenburg, on the estate of an ignorant landowner who had red hair and the face of fox, and whom everyone treated with abject obsequiousness. I was his assistant gardener. But not for long.

The brand-new German republic needed me to help put down the workers' revolt in the Ruhr, so once again I became a soldier, on this occasion in the Reichswehr. By now I was sixteen. Again I had a splendid time. I loved being in the Reichswehr. I wanted to stay for ever. But the moment we arrived in the Ruhr, it was all over. I was told I was too young to stay in the Reichswehr.

So I went to North Berlin and lived miserably in an asylum with hundreds of bedraggled refugees from the east. Not having German papers I could not get work, only odd jobs like being a houseboy in an old baron's apartment near the Eden Hotel in the west end, near the Zoo. The baron was senile. The cruel young baroness forced him to live in a sunless room in the back of the house, with a canary to keep him company, while she entertained her guests in front. That was the first time since I was eleven that I could witness the good life. The minute the baroness found a butler with proper references I was given notice. On my last evening I was asked to clean the silver. As I did so, an idea occurred to me. 'Why not take a few spoons with me?' I asked myself. 'She'll never notice!' Well, I didn't take any at first. I tossed and turned all night. I'd been grossly underpaid. Besides the few marks in my pocket, I had nothing. In the morning, I had the nerve to do it.

Of course I was caught right away, confronted by the baroness who had a surprising command of gutter language, denounced to the police, arrested, tried and sent to prison, for the first time. I can't remember how many times I've been there since. Once, I spent the night in the waiting room of the Anhalter Bahnhof, which you are not supposed to do unless you have a railway ticket. I might have got away with it if I'd had German nationality. I spent a week in jail. When I got out I returned to the life of a phony proletarian, among beggars, pimps and whores.

But then, very slowly and gradually, I slithered into the career which made me famous. It began when a nice man suddenly called me *Herr Graf* [Mr. Count]. I protested vehemently. He laughed and said, 'One is always the person one appears to be. Once, in Vienna, the old Baron von Rothschild called me *Herr Baron*. Since then I call myself Baron. Who's there to stop me?"

Just before Christmas 1922, during the inflation, I had an amazing stroke of luck. I was standing at a street corner, begging. It was pouring. A well-dressed man appeared out of nowhere. He looked like a foreigner. He was wiping his face with a handkerchief and looking for a cab. When he put on his gloves I noticed a diamond ring. I offered to find him a cab. A cab came. As he stepped in, he handed me three bank notes, not unusual during the inflation when they were worth next to nothing. But when I looked at them, I discovered they were three American dollars. Dollars! I suddenly had enough money in my hands to live like a prince.

Let's jump a few years. Last year, right here in Cologne, while I was living in a hole in somebody's basement, I ran into a Czech who was looking for a traveling tobacco salesman. I applied and got the job. I didn't make any money at all until I met someone who called himself Baron Korff. He told me not to be a fool and to present myself as Count von der Recke. I did so. Immediately my luck changed. An old titled gentleman who bought a box of cigars from me insisted I stay for dinner and meet his wife and children. After dinner he showed me his collection of Japanese bronzes. He was amazed by my knowledge of Japanese bronzes. 'What an enchanting dinner companion you are, Count,' he said. 'I hope you will honour us again soon.'

It did not take me long to turn into something

considerably more rewarding than a mere Count von der Recke. I became a member of the oldest Baltic nobility, a sadly dispossessed refugee from my proletarianized homeland. My business boomed even more. I was received everywhere. Once, at a dinner party, I was placed next to the Countess of Buxtehude. I found out later that I was given this honour because it had been rumoured I was a prince. When I tried to track this down I discovered the rumour had originated with a clairvoyant.

On a few social occasions I actually allowed people to address me as Your Highness. They were deeply honoured. But I was not really happy doing it. To exploit the gullibility of decent citizens struck me as profoundly immoral. I did not as yet grasp that by allowing them to treat me as a prince I was doing them a tremendous favour. I simply gave them what they wanted. Who was I to deprive them of the pride of consorting with a prince and of the bittersweet joys of nostalgia for the happy days before the war?

This first phase of my career as a *Hochstapler*, of an impostor, of a confidence man, this dress rehearsal, did not last long. I was exposed. Those who foamed most indignantly about my villainy were exactly the same people who had been my most obsequious admirers. I was tried, convicted and sent to this very prison, for three months. The state attorney expressed genuine sympathy for me and assured me that he will do anything he can to help me after I was released. The judge, too, expressed deep regret, but he hoped I understood he simply had no choice. Many of the faces I now see every day, during our wood-sawing sessions in the prison yard, are the same as last year's. When I got out, the attractive social worker who looked after me thought I would be offended if she offered me a new winter coat. I was not a bit offended. She also gave me a very expensive leather briefcase.

From Cologne I made my way to Erfurt, next door, practically, to Weimar. One evening, when I did not have a pfennig in my pocket, I was sitting in a hotel lobby, wondering who was to buy me dinner. I pretended to read a newspaper when the owner of the hotel, who for some reason thought I was a baron, approached me and said I looked bored. What about coming along with him to call on Professor Gerhard, the painter, who was having an exhibition in one of the rooms upstairs? Good idea, I said, and went up with him in the elevator. Professor Gerhard wore a velvet jacket, a pince-nez and an enormous straw hat. He talked incessantly. One of his pictures showed the most revered of all the kings of Prussia, Frederick the Great, in a church, listening to a *Te Deum*. He had just won the Seven Years' War.

'Every time I see this picture,' the painter said, 'I'm moved to tears.'

'Very nice, very nice,' I observed. If this great patriot had an inkling of Frederick's profound contempt for everything German, I thought to myself, he would have chosen another hero to worship.

Professor Gerhard and the owner of the hotel then had a short exchange of views, looking at me closely. In the elevator, on the way down, my friend, the owner of the hotel, said to me, 'Do you know who the professor thinks you are? He thinks you are Prince Wilhelm of Prussia, the heir to the throne.' Before I had a chance to respond to this information, the professor came down, out of breath, full of apologies, and said he had forgotten to ask me to sign my name in the guest book. Would I mind terribly? For a fraction of a second I weighed the risks, but then quickly decided this was too good an opportunity to miss. I took his fountain pen and wrote Wilhelm of Prussia, in the stiff, vertical handwriting of my new grandfather, Kaiser Wilhelm. Then I went back to my room and went to sleep.

When I came down the next morning, the lobby was full. 'There he is! Doesn't he look exactly like the Kaiser when he was a young man?'

'There he is! Doesn't he look exactly like Frederick the Great when he was a young man?'

To earn the right to treat ordinary people like worms, the way a Hohenzollern prince should, I had to dispel whatever residual doubts about my identity some skeptics might still have. Therefore, I went to the desk and very audibly asked the concierge to put in a call to my mother, the Crown Princess, in Cecilienhof-Potsdam. When the call came through I went to the telephone cell, closed the door and said to the flunky who answered that I was Count von

Hardenberg and wished to know whether His Royal Highness Prince Wilhelm happened to be there on a visit. Unfortunately he wasn't, I was told, but I was given his temporary address in Bonn, Franziskanerstrasse 2.

Within ten seconds everybody knew that I had placed a call to Cecilienhof-Potsdam and everybody knew what that meant. I was promptly given the royal suite. Somebody dug up an oil painting of the Crown Princess to put over my bed. Good, I said to myself, she will have to pay the hotel bill. I told the owner that I intended to stay a little longer than I had planned, but I was afraid I was not really properly equipped. All my clothes were at home in Potsdam, I said, and it was a bit complicated to have them sent. He promptly presented me with a trousseau he borrowed from his nephew, a man, evidently, of exemplary taste. He was about my size.

I stayed in Erfurt for a couple of weeks. I saw no reason not to accept an invitation from a self-made businessman who had bought a château near Gotha and asked me to do him the honour of being his guest. A few days later, to show my gratitude, I took him to the theatre. He was my guest in the royal box. The audience was far more interested in me than in whatever happened on the stage. During intermission, the clicking of heels, from hotel porters to senior Reichswehr officers, sounded like the rat-a-tat-tat of a machine-gun.

During the next few days the local newspapers covered every move I made. Fortunately, no major paper had as yet discovered me. I knew that sooner or later Prince Wilhelm was bound to get wind of this. The effort I made to postpone the inevitable was beginning to be a bit of a strain. Once or twice I thought I would turn myself in. But I was not ready yet.

I saw no reason to be rude to titled owners of châteaux who practically begged me on their knees for the honour of playing host to me, so many of them that I was going to be splendidly looked after for at least the next six months. However, there were problems. The Hohenzollern family is surprisingly large. At dinner parties I ran into several members, or people who pretended to be members. I had to make a superhuman effort not to slip up. I did, on at least one occasion. I confessed I was uncomfortable in Bonn because it was still occupied by the French. Which wasn't at all the case. But nobody noticed. A few times somebody said to me, 'Your Royal Highness, I've observed that you have a strangely Baltic accent. You must surely be aware of it. I find it a little puzzling.' I always had the same answer. 'When I was a cadet,' I would respond, 'I had many friends from Kurland. I happened to prefer their dialect to mine.'

I imagined clouds were gathering when, on the main street of Gotha, I turned around and saw the expression of innocent indifference on the face of a man examining a store window. This could only be a detective. A little later, at a reception, a senior officer of the security police, a Major von Lowitz, followed every move I made. I was convinced he was waiting for the right moment to pounce on me. I began rehearsing how I would behave when he would at last say, 'Herr Domela, you are under arrest.' After I had finished rehearsing I gave him a haughty smile. He clicked his heels. I never saw him again.

On another occasion, a few overdressed old dowagers with long turkey-necks held the late President Ebert responsible for losing the war, for the Kaiser losing his throne and for the Treaty of Versailles.

'On the contrary,' I said calmly, 'you owe it to him that he crushed the revolution for you. You owe it to him that you still have your estates, your servants and your money in the bank. And my father and his brothers and sisters and all other royal princes, whether in Saxony or Bavaria, owe it to him that they're not guests of the Salvation Army. Not as yet, anyway.'

The old ladies were aghast. They couldn't believe their ears. 'But Your Royal Highness,' they lamented, 'that you, of all people, should say such things—it's unbelievable!'

One day I heard that the man who looked after the finances at the Crown Prince's household in Potsdam was about to arrive. There could only be one reason for the visit. But no, he was on his way to Weimar to worship at Goethe's shrine.

All this was utterly nerve-wracking. Was it worth the trouble? Not really, but I was not quite ready yet I give myself up. Once I was ready, I would do it in my own time, on my own terms. This would be impossible once the Berlin papers began to cover my activities in Erfurt and Gotha. I devised a plot to prevent this.

I arranged a visit to the closest Reichswehr barracks. There, the commander in charge, with whom I had shared the odd bottle of wine, received me ceremoniously. I asked him whether he agreed with me that it would not be good for the republican image of the Reichswehr if the left-wing press in Berlin discovered that I was on friendly terms with senior officers. Could he use his influence with the press to keep this quiet?

It worked like a charm.

Soon the moment came for me to pull the chain. One day, the mayor of Erfurt invited me to inspect a factory. The visit was to begin at three in the afternoon. At quarter to three I was on the train going west. It did not take the police long to discover that I had been a phony prince. There were screaming headlines all over Germany. The entire police force was mobilized to catch me. Nobody caught me. Once I saw French occupation troops in Koblenz the idea occurred to me to join the Foreign Legion. Yes, that was the ideal solution. I managed to reach their facilities for a medical. If accepted I would have to sign up for five years, they said. A French doctor examined me and said I was too weak, I would be dead within two years. I pleaded with him. Germany had no use for me, I said, I would rather endure a terrible end than to return to a life of homelessness and shame. He yielded. The actual enlisting was to be done in Euskirchen, in the Verdun barracks, just this side of the French border. The police arrested me on the station platform in Euskirchen, just as I was about to step on the train.

After a month in prison I received a letter from my mother. She had not been killed in January 1920 after all, as I had been told eight years earlier, but had only been seriously wounded. She was alive and well in Kowno [Kaunas]. To her greatest joy she had learned about my whereabouts from the newspapers.

No one is better equipped than a real mother to help a phony prince find his feet again.

• • •

The Record

After being released from prison in 1927, Harry Domela went to Berlin. In 1933, he emigrated to Amsterdam, via Vienna and Paris. He fought as an officer on the republican side in the Spanish Civil War. From 1938 to 1940, he was in Antwerp. Later he was interned as an enemy alien in the French camp in Gurs. He managed to get out and reach Mexico, where he was arrested. He spent several years in camps in Jamaica. Somehow, under different names, he made his way to South America. He was born in 1904. He could still be alive.

A poster in the photograph of Harry Domela shows that a film was made of Der Falsche Prinz. A search through the reference books has so far been fruitless.

11

PETER'S GENEROUS HOST

On October 15, 1923, the government created the Rentenbank [German Mortgage Bank], which was to issue currency to be redeemable upon demand in interest-bearing gold mortgage certificates. Four weeks later, Rentenmarks became legal tender. Rampant inflation was brought under control. Hjalmar Schacht was appointed National Currency Commissioner. In December he became president of the Reichsbank.

The year 1923 was the *annus horribilis* of the Weimar republic. Between the time the Rentenbank was established and the day, four weeks later, the Rentenmark became legal tender, Hitler staged his beer hall putsch in Munich. Radicals of the Left threatened the republic in Saxony and Thuringia. In the Ruhr, there was passive resistance against the French occupation.

Not least because he assured himself from the beginning of the sympathy and support of British financial circles, Schacht was successful. London was opposed to the French policy of extracting reparations by force.

Schacht also counted on American help.

Excerpt from Peter's diary:

<u>Wednesday, October 30, 1929</u>
Alphonse gave me a worldly-wise smile when I dropped in to pick up the Charlie Chaplin brooch before lunch. It was perfect. He found a suitable green leather case for it and sent me on my way.

Brigitte was waiting for me at Kempinsky's, looking enchanting, her eyes more limpid than ever. I'd forgotten to reserve a table, but the maître d' recognized me and gave us a suitably quiet spot at the back. My two guardians, Hans Bräutigam and Egon Martens, protected us while having a beer in the bar.

After I ordered the wine, I gave Brigitte the green leather case.

She held her breath as she opened it.

She was speechless.

"Every girl should have an American millionaire like you!" she exclaimed once she had regained her speech and planted a big kiss on my cheek. "As long as he comes from Berlin. All problems would be solved. When I come and visit you in America, will you introduce me to Charlie? I promise I'll wear the brooch."

"Of course," I said.

"And will you be jealous if we have an affair?"

"Not for a moment," I replied. "We don't allow jealousy in America. We think it's a German vice."

"We're certainly good at it. The only thing that's not rotten in this country is the Kurfürstendamm."

"Is that why you think Adolf Hitler is right about a lot of things?"

There was an abrupt change of mood. "I knew you were going to grill me about this." She became very upset. "Always testing. I bet you couldn't wait. I'm surprised you didn't talk about Adolf Hitler all night."

"I had other things to do."

That brought a faint smile to her face.

"And you did them superbly."

"Thank you." I would not relent. "Now, please answer my question."

"Are you a spy for somebody?"

"No, Brigitte, I'm not a spy," I said grumpily. "But it is true that I take Hitler more seriously than other Americans do. As a matter of fact, I wouldn't be surprised if I'm the only American who takes him seriously. There's nothing sinister about it at all."

"If you really want to know what I think," she replied, "I'll be happy to tell you. Are you ready? All right. I've never heard him speak. He's only been here once, and I didn't bother. I hear he's great speaker but I don't care about that. I like him because I think that he's being logical. It's as simple as that. He's obviously right that the political system we have is a mess. And he's right when he says that we were no more responsible for the war than the others. And that the people who signed the Treaty of Versailles for Germany are traitors. And so are the people who are in favour of going on and on and on paying reparations until doomsday. And that the time has come for us to take matters into our own hands. And that those who're against him are on the side of the people who want to enslave us."

"Did you say enslave us?" I asked.

"Yes, that's what I said."

"That, my dear, doesn't sound like a word you use in ordinary conversation. It sounds like somebody else's word. Do you know any Nazis?"

"I knew you were going to ask me, sooner or later." Now she was furious. "Fritz Wagner confessed to me he told you about my friend Horst Zahlendorf."

"Who's Fritz Wagner?"

"Our UFA driver. Don't you remember?"

"Of course." I had really forgotten. "You don't have to talk about Zahlendorf unless you want to," I said.

"Well," she snapped, "the truth is I don't want to talk to you about him. Do you still want to take me to *Die Fledermaus* on Friday?"

For a moment I hesitated.

Then I said, in a voice more sorrowful than hopeful, "Yes I do."

Notes

Scene: Hjalmar Schacht's private library on the same floor as my suite in the Reichsbank. He and I were sitting on leather chairs near a desk.

I thanked him for his generous hospitality. He expressed the Reichsbank's wish that I stay as long as I liked.

We talked about the Young Plan.

"I might as well tell an old friend like you, Peter," he said, "that my wife Luise is very angry with me for signing it." I glanced at a photograph of Frau Dr. Schacht on the desk, a formidable round-faced lady looking considerably older than her husband.

"Isn't she aware of what would happen if you had not signed?" I asked. "Doesn't she know that a lot of the good work that's been done to admit you people again into decent society would have been undone if you hadn't signed? That the French would have continued their occupation of the Rhineland? That this would have been disastrous specially now that we're all facing hard times?"

"No, my friend. She does not know any of that. She does not listen to me. She listens only to Adolf Hitler. She thinks I am an accomplice in a plot to enslave the German people."

"I see," I said, full of understanding.

"I must ask you to keep this under your hat. I need not tell you that Luise no longer has any influence on what I do. She happens to have inherited from her father a narrow Prussian outlook. Alas, this condition has occasionally an unfortunate tendency to develop into bigotry. That's what makes her so receptive to the Far Right. Though, as far as I can see, there isn't a single Prussian in Hitler's entourage, and there's certainly nothing Prussian about him."

"Has your wife read *Mein Kampf*?"

"Of course."

"And you?"

"I've only been able to skim it and shudder. It's written by a semi-literate. A man without a clue about economics. That's bad enough, but the book is also an assault on the German language. Hardly more than 10 percent of those who own a copy can have read it. Why are you asking?"

"Because I've gone through it rather carefully. Please forgive me, Hjalmar, but I have quite a different reaction. I think Hitler is the coming man. Once the crisis really starts and the German economy collapses, we Americans will call in our loans and won't lend you Germans another dime, not even to keep the communists out. Soon thereafter the Nazis will be big in the Reichstag and in the country. No other party will be able to form a government. President Hindenburg will turn to Hitler to take over."

Schacht closed his eyes.

"To be quite frank with you, Peter," Schacht said, his voice trembling, "such a possibility has never occurred to me. What a nightmare! Sometimes, in the middle of the night, I have had quite a different dream, not a nightmare at all, something I can easily live with. Are you listening?"

"I'm listening."

"I have dreamed that if the republic arrives at an impasse, as I agree is most likely, we'll restore the monarchy and put one of the Kaiser's sons on the throne. You see, Peter, we don't know how to play the republican game. We prefer a man on top. Monarchy, I've always thought, is the natural form of government for Germany. But I don't expect an American like you to agree with that. Even an American from Berlin."

"You're right. What about the British way—a democratic monarchy?"

"No. We have no talent for democracy. We never agree on anything. The worst people always prevail. Look at the way this government has treated me. Again and again I've told them it's suicidal to borrow American billions in foreign exchange, which we then pay to our former enemies in reparations. We're supposed to pay reparations out of the revenues earned through exports, not by borrowing. Borrowing is a recipe for disaster. We can't pay reparations out of exports because the Versailles treaty has made it impossible for us to earn enough money from exports to pay the reparations and still have enough left over to live on." Schacht became increasingly agitated as he continued. "This cannot change unless they amend the treaty. Borrowing merely creates an artificial boom. It's ruinous for many other reasons as well. It makes our unemployment much worse than it would otherwise be. We can only use the borrowed money to pay reparations or to purchase foreign goods. This means that we put many home producers out of business. It's an immoral policy that is, of course, to the politicians' short-term advantage. That's the trouble with borrowing. When I tell them, they turn the other way. At every international conference I attend, they undercut me. After I signed the Young Plan, the government knowingly and deliberately kept me in complete ignorance of the concessions it had made behind my back, contrary to the terms of our arrangements. I don't think I can stand it much longer."

"Even if they listened to you and acted accordingly," I said, "and even if every member of the Reichstag was as intelligent and high minded as you are, Hjalmar, Germany would still be in deep trouble during the coming depression. No country will be immune."

Schacht was deep in thought. Then he took off his pince-nez and looked at me.

"You can't be serious about Hitler, are you?"

"Oh yes, absolutely."

"One of the things I find most objectionable in him," Schacht said, "is his anti-Semitism. He wants to exclude Jews from any role in Germany whatsoever. That's idiotic! I can't imagine our people ever supporting such a policy. Imagine running an economy without Jews. No, this is simply another measure of his economic illiteracy. The Nazi Party's platform of 1920 says something quite different. It guarantees Jews the same rights as foreigners—by implication the same rights German citizens enjoy abroad. There's nothing in the Party program, or any other Party manifesto, that suggests that Jews will ever be denied the right to do business, to practice as doctors, work as teachers, manage estates, and so on. *Mein Kampf*, on the other hand, demands the elimination of Jews from German society altogether. That's in direct conflict with the Party platform. It would mean a direct violation of basic legal principles. Have you seen the Party program?

I had not. But I heard later that the Nazi party's conference in Bamberg in February 1926 had decided that the Führer's wishes were henceforth to prevail over the Party program. This was one of the first formal steps towards the creation of a *Führerpartei*.

"Well," Schacht resumed, "most of its demands can be readily accepted by any party. The Party simply wants the best for the greatest possible number, that's all. You must remember, Peter, that National Socialism first appeared on the political scene simply as a national movement. Many people naturally prefer it to communism, whose adherents dance to Moscow's tune. Also, the Party program supports religion, the maintenance of property and the encouragement of private enterprise. And it puts great emphasis on personal values."

I looked at my watch.

"You seriously think, Hjalmar," I asked as I rose, "the Party program will prevail over *Mein Kampf* once they come to power?"

He took me to the door and slapped me on the back.

"Don't worry about that for a single moment, Peter. They won't."

The Record

Soon after Hitler came to power he chose Hjalmar Schacht to serve him as Minister of Economics. Schacht did so from 1934 and 1937, and, using his own version of Keynesianism, put an end to the depression and masterminded Hitler's rearmament. Later he quarreled with the Nazis, and towards the end of the war spent some time in a concentration camp. In 1946, at Nuremberg, he was indicted as a war criminal. He was acquitted. After the war he was active as an economic expert in the Near and Far East. He died in 1970.

12

ISIDOR

Joseph Goebbels, aged thirty-two, was Hitler's *Gauleiter* in Berlin. In September 1928, his paper *Der Angriff* [The Attack] launched a campaign against the Dawes Plan. Goebbels had no idea what the Dawes Plan was and confessed to his colleagues that he was not in the least interested. All he knew was that it had something to do with paying reparations.

'What does the Dawes Plan mean?' *Der Angriff* asked. Taking each letter in 'Dawes,' the paper provided the answer: *'Deutschlands Armut Wird Ewig Sein'* [Germany's poverty will last for ever]. For the anti-Dawes campaign a special party emblem was invented, showing the German people as slaves under the Dawes cross, with a clenched fist as a symbol of resistance. A Dawes Week was launched in which Goebbels, addressing Party meetings in the suburbs of Berlin, roused the rabble by railing against the exploiters of the 'Dawes Colony.'

One target of his attack was the *'Vipoprä,'* a nickname for the 'Vice-President of Police,' a position held by Dr. Bernhard Weiss. He was the first unbaptized Jew ever employed in the higher echelons of the Prussian public service. Weiss had earned the Iron Cross First Class in the war, and was an exemplary official.

He had been a member of the Berlin political police since May 1918, chief from 1920 to 1924, subsequently chief of the criminal police and, finally, since 1927, vice-president of the Berlin police. In this capacity he commanded 14,000 truncheon-wielding uniformed policemen.

Goebbels called him Isidor, a name frequently used by anti-Semites to insult Jews. This was rather strange because it is a Greek name, not a Hebrew or Yiddish one, meaning the gift of Isis. In the case of Bernhard Weiss, Goebbels used it not merely to insult but to destroy.

Excerpt from Peter's diary:

<u>Wednesday, October 30, 1929</u>

At seven I met Bernhard in his office at the police's red-brick headquarters, *Die Rote Burg* [The Red Fortress], on the Alexanderplatz, the subject of Alfred Döblin's extraordinary new novel *Berlin Alexanderplatz*. I had not read it yet, but I knew it told a pitiful story of an unemployed man by the name of Franz Biberkopf. The fortress was called red not only because the bricks were red. No, this was the centre of Red Berlin. It was certainly no coincidence that the imperial police had been housed here, in the middle of enemy territory.

Could it be, I thought, that it was only two days ago that I made the entry in this diary about Berlin's two west ends, Brigitte's Kurfürstendamm and Frederick the Great's Unter den Linden, which included the Hohenzollerns' palace and Hjalmar Schacht's Reichsbank? I had now left behind both west ends, including my own birthplace in Wilmersdorf and Gertrud's Tiergarten, as well as the Brandenburger Tor, not to mention the busiest traffic centre in Europe, the Potsdamer Platz—the intersection of six major streets that made history because it had produced the first traffic light in Berlin. I had moved along Unter den Linden to the geographical centre of Berlin, which happens to be sociologically directly connected to Wedding and Neukölln I had toured yesterday with Edwin Rehberg.

The Alexanderplatz, Franz Biberkopf's 'Alex,' was the site of a large complex of police buildings that included law courts and a prison. In November 1918 revolutionary workers took the prison and liberated six hundred and fifty political prisoners. I had heard that the Kaiser's Alexandriner Dragoner made excellent use of that very moment to change sides and join the revolution, the first Berlin regiment to do so. I remember very well the excitement with which I followed these events. A few weeks later, on January 12, 1919, the social democratic commander-in-chief of the brand-new republic, Gustav Noske crushed the last attempt by workers' and soldiers' councils to seize power, in a bloody encounter right here.

I was delighted to see Bernhard in top form.

"I've a lot to tell you, Peter," he said. As always, he spoke in his strong Berlin dialect. I knew that his enemies often made fun of his diminutive size. He stood five foot four.

"Look," he pointed to a side table, "I've done my homework. These are the things I want you to see. But first, how are you? Any more nasty letters?"

"No, no more nasty letters, thank you. Your security men may have told you that I've thrown myself at the mercy of Hjalmar Schacht and taken refuge in the Reichsbank."

"Oh yes, I forgot. Certainly one of the safer 'hotels' in Berlin."

We walked over to the side table.

"Look at this."

He opened a file marked *Der Angriff*, and pointed to a cartoon dated January 16, 1928, showing a huge St. Bernard dog with a stormtrooper between his teeth, on his way to a prison named 'St. Bernhard.' Over the prison door was the standard caricature of a Jew—curly hair, low forehead, horn-rimmed glasses, crooked nose, no chin, big flapping ears.

"You see, they got the point," Bernhard said. "I hit back the moment they hit me. I don't let them get away with a thing. I've already banned the Party once. I'll do it again and again, as often as is necessary. You watch me—I'll crush them. Look at this book, *Das Buch Isidor*."

I leafed through a collection of cartoons and articles. When Weiss's real first name Bernhard was used it was put in quotation marks. Even the crossword puzzles often contained the name 'Isidor.' One cartoon showed a bespectacled, big-nosed donkey splay-legged on thin ice with the face of Isidor. Another presented Isidor asking a policeman who demanded the arrest of a communist thug: 'Ban them—why? Did he attack a Jew?' Another, with the caption 'Rejoice, Daughter of Zion,' showed a smiling Isidor admiring a Christmas tree decorated with hanged stormtroopers. In the most devastating cartoon of all, with the caption 'His Ash Wednesday will come, too,' swastika flags are blowing in the wind and Isidor sits in the gutter under a street lamp, a rope around his neck.

"A clear case of defamation." Bernhard tried to keep his voice under control. "Of course I brought action."

"I suppose the judge was on Goebbels' side," I said.

"Not exactly, but not on mine either. One of the difficulties is that Goebbels is one of the twelve Nazis in the Reichstag and has immunity. He has nothing but contempt for the Reichstag, of course, and he boasts about being an *I.d.I.*, *Inhaber der Immunität* [a possessor of immunity], as though it was the Iron Cross. During the election campaign in 1928 he promised that the Nazis who were running for office would not become parliamentarians but would remain revolutionaries. They would pursue a policy of infiltration, in order to destroy from within. Good thing they received only 2.6 percent of the vote."

I asked him whether he ever scored any convictions.

"Not often enough," he responded vehemently. "But by God, I try hard. Last year we'd banned the Party for a few months. In that time I hauled stormtroopers before the magistrate every day, for wearing the forbidden brown shirts and for endangering peace and security. And I subpoena the editors of *Der Angriff* responsible for the Isidor business whenever I can. The defence is always that Isidor is not an individual, not a person in the legal sense. To describe me as a Jew could not be defamatory, the Nazis argue, since I have never denied being a Jew. They say the name 'Isidor' 'alludes to a collective concept intended to criticize the prevailing Judaization of leading positions in Prussia' and was fair comment.

"How do Goebbels' people behave in court?"

"They play to the gallery. They treat it as a joke and say Berliners love a joke. They say I'm generously giving them free publicity. And the press accuses me of not having a sense of humour. Let's go and eat. I'll tell my driver we'll be back at nine. I hope you don't mind that one of my men will follow us."

"Really?"

"I don't take unnecessary risks. I'm not exactly Berlin's most popular citizen."

The weather was mild and it was getting dark as we walked along the noisy Alexanderstrasse, the poor man's Kurfürstendamm. On the way, at my insistence, we looked in at a crowded dance hall—the entrance fee was seventy pfennige—and watched girls (most of them evidently office or shop girls during the day, some not so young) in bathing costumes dancing with men in street clothes to the tune of *Was machst Du mit dem Knie, lieber Hans, mit dem Knie, lieber Hans, beim Tanz?* [What are you doing with your knee, dear Hans, while dancing?] In the centre of the small dance-floor the master of ceremonies, a chain of fake military decorations around his neck, barked commands through a megaphone. "Dance on the spot! If you move, you pay a round of beer for all!" All the tables had telephones, so guests could invite strangers at other tables to dance with them. It all seemed to be good, clean fun, mock-polite and a little old-fashioned.

Nobody recognized 'Isidor.' We left and turn into a side street. A table was waiting for us at Bernhard's favourite restaurant Beim Lindenbaum. He waved a greeting to the policeman in civvies who had followed us and sat down at a separate table. The waiter obviously liked Bernhard and called him Herr Doktor. We ordered pork chops and a bottle of red wine.

Notes

"I am, of course, God's gift to Goebbels," Bernhard said. "A Jew who looks the part."

"Don't you also get threatening letters?"

"Dozens. I don't tell my wife. So far they've left her alone, thank God."

"Have you read *Mein Kampf*?"

"I have my hands full with Goebbels," Bernhard replied. "One Nazi at a time. Last November Hitler came to Berlin for the first time, after the ban was lifted. He spoke at the Sportpalast. This is really a red city, so it's not easy for him. One of the stormtroopers, a man by the name of Kütemeyer, one of the cashiers, got drunk and on the way home, fell into the Landwehrkanal and drowned. My police haven't been able to find out exactly what happened. The Nazis need martyrs. So Goebbels made a big noise and claimed that a simple man who wanted to experience for the first time the solemn, life-enhancing joy of hearing his Führer speak was beaten to death on his way home."

"Not bad," I said.

"You're right, Peter. Not bad. And right now, during Hugenberg's and Hitler's campaign against the Young Plan, he's pulling out all the stops. He simply repeats all the slogans he'd made up to fight the Dawes Plan and applies them to the Young Plan. He rants about Young-slavery, and shouts Germany is being turned into a Young-colony. Do you know what he wrote the other day?"

Bernhard took a clipping from his wallet.

"He had a religious upbringing, in Rheidt, not far from Cologne, and he loves biblical language and often sounds like a preacher. But sometimes he gets things a little mixed up. Listen. 'Germans have passed through the many stations of Golgatha and now their hangman, with mocking laughter, nails them to the cross.'"

"And what does he think about Hitler's new allies, Hugenberg and the Conservatives?"

"Good question!" Weiss finished his glass. "Goebbels used to be a struggling young bohemian intellectual. He has always been a socialist rather than a nationalist. He hates the bourgeoisie more than anything else. Before he read *Mein Kampf* in the fall of 1925 he was no more anti-Semitic than anybody else. The main enemy was the bourgeoisie, not the Jews. But since he read *Mein Kampf* he's found anti-Semitism useful, very useful."

"I have a suggestion, Bernhard," I said. "Leave all this. Come to New York. I'll get you a job as an MC in a night club. Or maybe as security man down in Wall Street."

Bernhard shook his head vigorously.

"Sorry, Peter," he declared without a smile. "That's very nice of you. Thank you. But I'll never give up. I'm going to stay right here. You'll see—we'll beat them. The republic is doomed if we don't fight back. I have a job to do."

The Record

When Goebbels was Minister of Propaganda and Enlightenment in Hitler's government he sometimes spoke about Bernhard Weiss. What a marvelous experience it had been, he remembered with pride, to transform 'Isidor' into 'the most brutal bailiff of the Weimar republic, into the grinning mask of the eternal Jew,' when 'he was actually only a harmless fool.'

In July 1932, during a right-wing coup in the State of Prussia that served as a dress rehearsal for things to come, Bernhard Weiss was summarily dismissed. He had no time to gather up his bowler hat and pince-nez before being driven to prison from his headquarters on the Alexanderplatz in an army Mercedes. In due course he was released. In 1933, he fled to London via Czechoslovakia. In 1937 he was stripped of his German citizenship 'for having promoted the immigration of eastern Jews into Germany.'

Two years later, he was in London when war broke out. In 1914, all German nationals who lived in England, or happened to be there, were automatically interned, as were British nationals in Germany. But in September 1939, the situation was complicated because there were about 60,000 German and Austrian 'enemy aliens' in Britain who, although technically still enemy aliens, were in fact refugees. It was out of the question to treat them as though they were Nazis. The government solved this problem by establishing tribunals to sift out those who were immediate security risks and those who were not. In the case of Bernhard Weiss, a gross mistake was made. For some reason, the tribunal decided he was a Nazi. Weiss was immediately interned, together with a Nazi whom he had arrested in Berlin ten years earlier. The mistake was soon cleared up and he was treated like the rest of the refugees.

After the war, Weiss managed a stationery and printing enterprise until he died in 1951.

13

A TELEGRAM AND A VISIT

On Thursday morning, just before breakfast, Peter received a telegram from Charlie Chaplin.

HOW FORTUNATE YOU'RE IN BERLIN JUST WHERE I NEED YOU STOP AS YOU KNOW AM WORKING ON FILM TO BE CALLED CITY LIGHTS STOP PROBABLY MY LAST SILENT FILM STOP I CALL IT A COMEDY ROMANCE IN PANTOMIME STOP SCRIPT READY CASTING COMPLETE WITH EXCEPTION ONE SECONDARY CHARACTER STOP I WANT SAME TYPE AS LOUISE BROOKS STOP YOU MET HER AFTER GOLDRUSH OPENING NEW YORK STOP DON'T WANT ASK LOUISE HERSELF FOR REASONS YOU CAN GUESS STOP YOU PROBABLY HAVE UFA CONTACTS STOP DO I HAVE A CHANCE STOP NO ENGLISH REQUIRED STOP GREETINGS CHARLIE

I sent Charlie a short reply assuring him I would do my best.

Excerpt from Peter's diary:

<u>Thursday, October 31st, 1929</u>
How nice of Charlie to have put a potent weapon into my hands!

What price can I exact from Brigitte in return for sending her to Hollywood? Can I say to her, 'I will give Charlie your name if you arrange with your stormtrooper to leave me alone and make sure his friends follow his lead?'

After breakfast I went back to my room to think this through. I did not get very far before the telephone rang. The valet who looked as though he had served General Ludendorff at army headquarters was on the line. A gentleman was downstairs, he announced, waiting to see me.

"Did he give his name?" I asked.

"Yes. Horst Zahlendorf."

I do not like coincidences on the stage, in the movies or in novels. I always think the author is being lazy. But when they happen in real life, I don't dare call the Power That Pulls The Strings lazy. I meekly submit. The question was not why Zahlendorf should turn up just now. The question was how did he know I was here?

I did some quick thinking.

"Are my security men in the building?"

"Yes, sir. Officers Hans Bräutigam and Egon Martens have been given rooms on the top floor. I happen to know they are there now."

"Please ask them whether they would be so kind as to come down and ask this gentleman what he wants. In the meantime he'll have to be patient."

But he wasn't patient at all. While the gold-braided valet was on the phone, Zahlendorf, obviously an experienced operator, found the stairs and walked up. He spotted my suite without difficulty. Feeling reasonably safe in the bank, I had left my door slightly ajar. He gently pushed it open and walked in. I was still sitting at the telephone table.

Zahlendorf seemed indistinguishable from any minor bank official who might be working at a desk downstairs. He wore a raincoat, carried a grey fedora hat and wore a light beige suite and a tie.

"Good day, Herr Zahlendorf," I made my voice sound neutral. "I know who you are." I did not offer him a seat.

"Good day, Mister Hammersmith," he said. "You need not waste your time asking me how I found you. We have many friends at police headquarters. They all give you the highest marks for choosing the Reichsbank as your refuge from the Adlon. It's convenient to have good connections when one thinks one needs them."

He looked around with mock admiration. "Very nice," he said and whistled through his teeth. "I've never been backstage in a bank before. Hajum Schachtl certainly did well for himself."

"Who?" I asked.

"Hajum Schachtl, from Budapest. Or, if you prefer, Chaim Schachtl." I stared at him.

"You need not ask why I came to see you," he said. "I'll tell you in a minute. Nor do you need to call your two security guards, Hans Bräutigam and Egon Martens. You see, I am well informed. For the moment you're perfectly safe. And I prefer not to have any witnesses to what I am about to say. It'll take less than two minutes."

"Go ahead." I looked at my watch.

"Mister Hammersmith, you're known as a man of exceptionally good judgement. It does not surprise me that you prefer Brigitte to her colleague, Marlene Dietrich. I just don't want you to misunderstand the situation. Brigitte is ambitious. She'll fake anything to please a man she thinks can be useful to her. That's one of the many things I've taught her. I know the only man who counts with her is me. She'll do anything I say. You are a Berliner yourself so you know we Berliners are civilized people. I encourage her to entertain whomsoever she likes."

He paused. I said nothing.

"Obviously I have nothing against Brigitte having other friends, rich or poor. But we prefer them rich. But I won't have her go out with Jews."

I closed my eyes. I would rather bite my tongue than reply to that.

"Does Brigitte know you're here?" I asked.

"I think you should try and figure that out yourself."

He put his hand in the pocket of his raincoat and picked out Alphonse Friedberg's Charlie Chaplin brooch.

"All I'll tell you is that Brigitte does not accept presents from Jews. Give the brooch to Charlie Chaplin when you return to America. He'll be delighted to give it to one of the many Aryan girls he's screwing. I've often wondered why you Jews don't pick your own kind."

I reached for the telephone.

"Don't bother," Zahlendorf said. "I'm going anyway. Just let me tell you one more thing, Mister Hammersmith. If you see Brigitte again, you will not return to America alive. We will have to send the brooch to Charlie Chaplin by mail."

14

THE LAST CHANCE

Peter's appointment with the left-wing social democrat Paul Levi was at ten on Thursday morning, in his office in the Reichstag. The American ambassador Jacob Gould Schurman had told him that Levi was the most eloquent defence lawyer in Germany, a former communist who had tangled with Lenin, a great friend of Rosa Luxemburg's whom he revered, and perhaps even her lover.

Peter was curious to meet Levi. Ernst Toller had presented to him the position of a playwright who had no faith in political parties blocking Hitler. Now Peter had a chance to meet a man who was active in day-to-day party politics and was therefore likely to have a different approach.

The German communists, Edwin Rehberg had told Peter the previous day, followed Stalin's line. Their main enemies were the social democrats, whom they called 'social fascists,' not the Nazis. If Rehberg was correct, the chances of the parties of the Left uniting against Hitler were nil. On the Left, therefore, the only combined action possible was by the unions. This was what Ernst Toller hoped. It struck Peter as utopian.

But there was also a force on the Right that could stand in Hitler's way: the Conservatives, perhaps in conjunction with the Reichswehr. He would find out more about that this afternoon when he saw General Kurt von Schleicher.

But perhaps Rehberg was not right. Perhaps, when the Moment of Truth came, the German communists would defy Moscow. Before the war, their two founders, Rosa Luxemburg and Karl Liebknecht, had broken with the leadership of the German Social Democratic Party, which they considered too moderate, and had taken radical positions. In August 1914, they formed the Spartacus League, which was dedicated to ending the war through revolution. In 1918, the Spartacus League evolved into the Communist Party of Germany. During the revolution in November 1918, Luxemburg and Liebknecht were released from prison and immediately demanded political power for the workers' and soldiers' soviets that were being formed.

Rosa Luxemburg, born in Poland, had been an outstanding left-wing intellectual and a dynamic speaker. In 1913 and 1914, she had chosen Paul Levi, not yet thirty and already active in radical politics, to defend her in a number of cases brought against her for seditious, anti-military activities.

In 1915, Levi was drafted and sent to the Western front, but after going on a hunger strike he managed to obtain a discharge and to make his way to Zürich where one of his sisters lived. There he was politically active, helping kindred spirits desert from the German army. He was with Lenin early in 1917 when news reached Zürich about the outbreak of revolution in Russia and he was among the well-wishers who sent Lenin off as he left in a sealed train across Germany on his famous journey to Finland Station in St. Petersburg.

Throughout the war he and Rosa Luxemburg, who spent some of the war years in prison in Breslau, remained in contact. Their correspondence dealt with the wide range of subjects that interested them in addition to politics—birds, plants and rocks. Lenin's friend Karl Radek called Paul Levi 'a psychological puzzle, full of contradictions, deeply preoccupied with ancient vases and the Pyramid of Cheops, responsible for much fruitless skepticism in the Party.

Rosa Luxemburg had always been a believer in democracy and fought valiantly against Lenin's dictatorial and terrorist methods. At the same time she, like Ernst Toller, opposed any form of parliamentary government, as incompatible with the interests of the working class. Inevitably, it would be dominated by the bourgeoisie and therefore 'anti-proletarian.'

In November 1918, before she and Liebknecht could assume effective leadership, they were forced into hiding when officers of the Freikorps conducted a manhunt; the pair were in an apartment in, of all places, bourgeois Wilmersdorf. They may have been betrayed by the minor Communist Party worker Wilhelm Pieck, who later became the first president of Communist East Germany. On January 15, 1919, they were brought to headquarters at the Eden Hotel, beaten with rifle butts and then taken away to be driven—so it appeared—to Moabit prison. On the way they were shot to death. Later, it was claimed they were trying to escape while under arrest. The troopers took Rosa Luxemburg's body to the Liechtenstein Bridge and dropped it in the Landwehr Canal.

After the murder of Karl Liebknecht and Rosa Luxemburg, Levi became one of the leaders of the Communist Party. This meant repeated visits to Moscow to attend congresses. In March 1921, he took issue with Lenin's line that the German and other non-Russian communist parties had no choice but to submit to Moscow's authority.

He was expelled.

Soon after he joined the social democrats.

Excerpt from Peter's diary:

<u>Thursday, October 31, 1929</u>

I was fifteen when the Reichstag building was inaugurated. 'Beauty is educational,' the Kaiser declared in his speech at the opening ceremony. He was referring to the Reichstag's Italian High Renaissance architecture. It was the function of art, he announced, to have an uplifting effect on the Volk, the people.

I remember the jokes some of us *l'art pour l'art* aesthetes made about that speech during recess in the Fichte Gymnasium. Whatever beauties he'd seen, someone said, they certainly didn't have an educational effect on him.

This came back to me as I spotted the imperial coat-of-arms in the gable of the Reichstag on my way to see Paul Levi. How symbolic! Unlike the Kaiser's bust as Emperor Augustus in the Adlon Hotel, which was awaiting resurrection in the basement, it survived the revolution in its original position, unscathed.

A venerable guard, who told me he was, like President Hindenburg, a veteran of the Franco-Prussian War, shepherded me along an endless corridor to Paul Levi's office. I was anxious to meet the Keeper of Rosa Luxemburg's Flame.

Yesterday, in the car, Rehberg showed me a private letter about Levi's memorable performance in a military court in the case against the judge who allowed Rosa Luxemburg's murderers get off practically scot-free. Albert Einstein was quoted as saying that it was 'uplifting to see how a single person committed to justice, equipped with the necessary sharpness of mind, has cleansed the atmosphere totally—a marvelous counterpart to Zola. Among the best of us Jews there is still something of the passion for social justice pervading the Old Testament.'

Paul Levi would refer to this case towards the end of our conversation.

He was clearly a man of refined tastes. While waiting for him to come in I admired his pictures on the wall, Greek temples and a Käthe Kollwitz print of a sad, thin-faced little girl in a grimy slum. On a small side table was a collection of Egyptian sculptures and near the window an exotic plant that looked like a miniature palm tree sprouted pink orchids. On his desk stood a photograph of a smiling woman in a pre-war dress in the middle of a meadow, wearing a hat with a wide rim covered with flowers, most likely Rosa Luxemburg.

Paul Levi entered and greeted me with Old World courtesy. He was a dignified, impressively tall middle-aged man with an unusually high forehead who spoke in a resonant baritone voice, no doubt highly effective in debate and in court. It was clear, and did not need to be said, that we shared the same humanistic ideals despite our different occupations. He told me he was well informed about my position on Wall Street.

I told him about my mission for Herbert Hoover.

Notes

> "I'm glad you alerted your president, Herr Hammersmith," Paul Levi said. "I'm by no means among those who underestimate Adolf Hitler. He knows it and he has singled me out in his speeches more than once as a particularly despicable specimen. Six years ago I wrote that any bold *condottiere* could easily break the fragile shell of our republic, and of course I meant him. As to your economic prognosis, Herr Hammersmith, I feel in my bones that you're right and that the whole world, but particularly Germany, faces a few very hard years. Yet I think Hitler can be stopped."
>
> "How?"

"By the joint action of our two workers' parties."

Everything I'd heard, I said, suggested that the division between them was by now too deep to make that possible. I'd been told repeatedly that under no circumstances would Stalin allow his German subordinates to cooperate with the social democrats.

"But Stalin may not be able to prevent it," Levi retorted, "once they begin to understand that he can't deal with his German comrades the way he deals with his peasant farmers with whom he's engaged in a life-and-death struggle. When Stalin consolidated his power after Lenin's death I knew we had another Genghis Khan on our hands. Once Hitler's alliance with the conservatives begins to pay off and he gains self-confidence, the leaders of the German communists will grasp very quickly that, Stalin notwithstanding, Hitler is their main enemy, after all, and not my party, the social democrats, whether Stalin calls us 'social fascists' or not. And it will appear absurd to them that Stalin regards Hitlerism merely as the final, imperialistic phase of capitalism, and that Hitler can easily be toppled should he comes to power, to make way for the Dictatorship of the Proletariat. No," he shook his head. "They will begin to understand that Hitler may very well destroy all opposition with a brutality of a kind we haven't had in Europe for a while and hold up the course of history for a century or two. As to your impression that our two parties are too far apart to be able to work together against a common enemy, you may not know, Herr Hammersmith, that they already have done so, quite effectively, in both Saxony and in Thuringia. It's all a question of leadership. No, Herr Hammersmith, I think you're far too pessimistic. The battle is by no means lost. The republic will survive."

I told him how delighted I was to hear him say this.

"I must add, however, that I don't regard the republic as a good *per se*. I know this may shock you, Herr Hammersmith. But I think the republic is merely the arena in which the class struggle is being fought out. The serious drawback of parliamentary democracy is that it tends to create illusions among the workers about their real position. My own party is now the leading member of the governing coalition together with the parties of the centre and the conservatives. I think join-

ing that coalition was a terrible mistake, and I've often said
so. It has happened once before that fatally misguided patriotism prevailed over the interests of the workers. In August 1914,
my party decided to support the war. That was an even greater
mistake—the same mistake, by the way, made by our French
friends. It seems that whenever we support, let alone join, a
bourgeois government we make compromises on fundamental
matters of principle, usually for disastrously wrong-headed
patriotic reasons. Power simply turns our heads. Imagine, we
even support bills for greater expenditures on armaments! The
parliamentary game creates illusions and tempts a working
man's party to join forces with class enemies. I realize that you
people in America don't use such language."

"We certainly don't," I agreed. "But I understand what
you are saying."

"If you look closely, our problems are not so different from
yours. The legacy of Rosa Luxemburg is that we cannot have
socialism without democracy, nor democracy without socialism. She was the one who came up with the formulation that
'freedom is always the freedom of the person who begs to dif-
fer.' That's the kind of thing I could imagine an American
politician saying, but not a Russian-style communist. That
was the real reason why Lenin and I parted ways. Our kind of
socialism is a child of the western Enlightenment, and not of
eastern autocracy and feudal absolutism."

"But isn't the ideal of a socialist republic," I asked, trying
hard not to show my bias against socialists, "very remote?"

"Not at all," Levi replied. "For a few short weeks after
November 1918 we had it. That was when the workers had
the power, and Rosa Luxemburg and Karl Liebknecht, after
they were released from prison, were their natural leaders. We
must never forget that the Weimar republic is really a creation
of the workers. But their spontaneous revolution was aborted
by the efficient and well-organized counter-revolution. Its main
weapon was cold-blooded, calculated murder, carried out sys-
tematically by officers of the Freikorps, the forerunners of the
Nazis. This was not just tolerated but encouraged by the government. Power slipped from the workers' hands. The revolution was only two months old when Rosa Luxemburg and
Karl Liebknecht were murdered. The slaughter continued in

Bavaria in February, and subsequently spread to many cities. Finally, nearly two and a half years later, it culminated in the assassination of Walther Rathenau."

I had a sudden itch at the back of my neck.

"I assume then that no more killings are to be expected," I said, my throat dry.

"Of course there will be more killings, " he replied with emphasis. "I have no doubt of that. There continues to be a great deal of violence in Germany. But fortunately the Freikorps have been dissolved. The nature of the killings has changed. Now that the Nazis have allied themselves with the militarist media-baron Alfred Hugenberg and his friends in big business, they will find new ways of getting rid of their enemies. While the administration of justice remains largely in the hands of nationalist judges there is no reason to assume that a determined Nazi with good connections in the judiciary may not be able to kill and escape punishment. Many judges adhere to the authoritarianism of the Kaiser's Germany and despise the republic."

This was far from new to me, but the expression on my face must have revealed that I was just a little disturbed.

"This seems to surprise you, Herr Hammersmith. I don't blame you. Let me tell you about the case on which I've been working for years. In 1919, a judge of a military court by the name of Paul Jorns deliberately allowed the murderers of Rosa Luxemburg and Karl Liebknecht to escape justice. He has since been promoted to a position on Germany's highest court. When an article appeared in the monthly *Das Tagebuch* in March of last year telling the truth about this horror, Paul Jorns sued for libel. I defended *Das Tagebuch* and won. Paul Jorns lodged an appeal. The case is coming up any moment now."

I told him how much I admired his spirit and his courage. Then I asked him what he thought will happen once the economy begins to collapse.

"Of course no one can predict how people will behave. Especially when we take into account human stupidity. I gave up complaining about it a long time ago. It's just as futile to call human beings stupid as it is to call the sun stupid because in the summer it shines too much and in the winter it does not shine enough. The current coalition cannot survive a crisis. It will break up. There will be a prolonged impasse. Now, let's assume for a moment people behave rationally. If they do, the Nazis will not be the beneficiaries of this impasse. The beneficiaries will be our two combined workers' parties. In terms of numbers, we, the proletariat, have an overwhelming majority. The situation may provide us with new revolutionary opportunities. This time we may succeed when last time we failed. The destructive work of the counter-revolution may be undone. I'm a practical politician, Herr Hammersmith. No one has ever accused me of shallow optimism. I count numbers. I analyze election results. I regard politics as a game of chess. I assume that people's behaviour is determined by their self-interests, that they behave rationally. By that I mean that in the end the workers will stick together, in which case Hitler will not have a chance. However, if the situation deteriorates to such an extent that people will be in despair and behave irrationally, then darkness will descend, first in Germany, then in the whole world. But..."

He hesitated for a moment, smiled and looked at me closely. "What school did you go to, Herr Hammersmith?"

"The Fichte Gymnasium."

"Do you remember your Latin?"

"Of course. My teacher was a drill sergeant in the grenadiers."

"Good. In that case I can say what I want to say without you thinking me an intellectual snob."

"Go ahead."

"*Dum spiro spero.*" [While I breathe, I hope.]

The Record

In February 1930, Paul Jorns' appeal came before the court. On the third day of the trial, Paul Levi became seriously ill with influenza. It soon developed into pneumonia. He endured six days and six nights of dangerously high temperatures. During the sixth night, the night of February 9, 1930, he asked the nurse attending him for a cup of tea. She went to the kitchen to make it. When she returned the bed was empty, the window open.

His shattered body was found below, on a spot a few hundred metres from the Liechtenstein Bridge from which, eleven years earlier, Rosa Luxemburg's

THE MAN WHO KNEW CHARLIE CHAPLIN

body had been thrown into the Landwehr Canal. What exactly happened has never been explained. He may deliberately have thrown himself out of the window, or he may have lost his balance in his delirium. There was no evidence that anybody pushed him. He was forty-nine.

Two themes ran through the obituaries: his love for Rosa Luxemburg and the truth that 'only death could break his spine.'

Jorns won the appeal on a technicality. After Adolf Hitler came to power he was appointed judge in Roland Freisler's People's Court, which took over from the ordinary courts to deal with 'political crimes.' It soon became the most dreaded tribunal in the land. When Jorns retired in 1937, Hitler wrote him a personal letter of thanks for his services.

Freisler was killed during the war when an American bomb demolished his courtroom during a trial.

ERIC KOCH

15

A POLITICAL GENERAL

A bestseller in 1920 was Oswald Spengler's *Prussianism and Socialism.* Spengler was the author of *The Decline of the West,* the first volume of which had appeared two years earlier. The point of the new book was that the Prussia of Frederick the Great, with its slogan 'To Each his Own,' had essentially been a socialist state. It had emphasized collectivity, hard work and austerity. The state, Spengler wrote, had instilled in its citizens the virtues of order and discipline. He divorced socialism from Marxism.

This was in line with the thinking of anti-communists on the Right who were willing to cooperate with Weimar coalitions in which socialists participated. (Others, like Hugenberg, refused.) The president of the republic, Field Marshall Paul von Hindenburg, elected in 1925, belonged into that category, and so did his protégé General Kurt von Schleicher. Like Frederick the Great, they believed that the ultimate authority in the state was the army.

Von Schleicher was a member of an old military family in Brandenburg and a graduate of the *Kriegsakademie* [War Academy]. One of his instructors was Wilhelm Groener, a man widely regarded as clear headed and relatively democratic, who considered him one of his most brilliant pupils and sometimes referred to him affectionately as 'my adopted son.' Von Schleicher served in the Third Foot Guards, Hindenburg's old regiment, and made friends with his fellow officer, Hindenburg's son Oskar. Von Schleicher was popular, amusing, an excellent talker, a great horseman and superb dancer.

At the outbreak of the war in 1914, Kurt von Schleicher, then thirty-two, joined the general staff and was put in charge of railways. The head of his department happened to be General Wilhelm Groener. Except for an episode at the Eastern front, von Schleicher served on the general staff throughout the war, cultivating his talent for politics. Some combat officers referred to him sneeringly as a *Schreibtischoffizier* [desk officer].

November 9, 1918, was the day that the Kaiser's abdication was announced. This was a week after rioting had begun in all the major cities and workers' and soldiers' council were being formed around the country. Groener was by then quartermaster-general. With von Schleicher at his side, he assured the new chancellor, the socialist Friedrich Ebert, that the High Command would be at the new government's disposal whenever it was needed. Ebert accepted the offer. The High Command would continue its functions, Groener assured the chancellor, until the troops had returned home. This would inevitably take a little time. Soon von Schleicher played an active role financing and organizing the Freikorps, to combat Bolshevism.

In 1921 and 1922, von Schleicher became a pivotal figure in the secret rearmament of the Reichswehr, in defiance of the Treaty of Versailles. He held discussions with the Soviet emissary Karl Radek in his flat on the Mathäikirchplatz. The subject was the training of Soviet specialists in Germany, and of German pilots in Russia. (Kurt von Schleicher was aptly named. In English the German verb *schleichen* means 'to sneak,' 'to crawl,' 'to slink'; in middle high German *slichen*; in middle English *sliken*.)

The election of Hindenburg in 1925 made it possible for many on the Right to become reconciled to the Weimar republic. In 1928, thanks in part to von Schleicher's influence, Groener came out of retirement to become Minister for the Reichswehr, enabling von Schleicher henceforth to act as confidential adviser to the Minister, as well as continuing his role as grey eminence to the president of the republic. Groener created for him a special *Ministeramt*, a ministerial office, a link between the armed forces, the political parties and civilian officials.

Excerpt from Peter's Diary:

Thursday, October 31, 1929

The Scharnhorst Klub was on the second floor of a small, unmarked, insignificant building around the corner from the Reichswehr Ministry on the Bendlerstrasse, overlooking the chestnut trees along the Landwehr Canal. A dignified butler guided me to my general, who quickly put away *The Times* and rose to greet his guest. In full dress uniform, but with his collar loosened, he had been sitting in isolation, his face away from the door, near a potted palm. A considerable number of other high officers were reading papers and smoking in other parts of the room, and there was almost complete silence. Some were drinking tea, others spirits. I saw not a single civilian. In one of the corners was a tiled porcelain oven, presumably manufactured in Frederick the Great's porcelain works in Potsdam.

Completely bald, with quick dark-blue eyes and a grey mustache, von Schleicher was impressive only when speaking, which he did with lively animation and expressiveness. In repose he looked like a middle-aged senior postal clerk looking forward to early retirement.

Notes

> "Ah," Kurt von Schleicher said, shaking my hand firmly, "I've been wanting to meet you since early 1918 when I first heard about you. Take a seat."
>
> "You did?"
>
> He pulled over a leather armchair for me.
>
> "You were in mid-Atlantic, on your way to give pep talks to French and British troops on our western front, which was not at all quiet at the time. The Kaiser thought you were a greater threat than General Pershing. Orders were given to all our U-boats to sink you. You were a millionaire from Berlin with influence on Wall Street. And considerably brighter than Pershing. An excellent target. "
>
> "They missed," I observed.
>
> "I'm very glad they did." Von Schleicher smiled. A true man of the world, I thought. Just as expected. "Your ambassador's people told me you were on a fact-finding mission for your president. Is that right?"
>
> "Not quite, general. I want opinions, not facts."
>
> "But you've already formed your opinion," Schleicher said, pulling a copy of the *Weltzeitung* from his pocket. He began to read aloud.
>
> "'…Of all the dangers to the republic, he considers Adolf Hitler a more serious danger than Alfred Hugenberg or the communists.' You want to know what I think of that?"
>
> "I do."
>
> "I'm not sure which I would prefer, catching the bubonic

plague or the cholera. I agree with you that we're facing bad times. They've already started. Both the Nazis and the communists will do uncomfortably well in the next election. Hugenberg will profit. But I don't quite agree with your view about the Nazis. After all, like most Germans they subscribe to the national idea. What harm is there in that? Aren't Americans great patriots as well? By the way, I understand the communists are not very popular in the United States either. Of course you're right, a lot will depend on the way we deal with the Nazis."

Obviously 'we' meant the Reichswehr.

"I'm not sure anyone can deal with them," I said, "once things get really rough."

"I'm afraid, Herr Hammersmith, you're far too pessimistic. You underestimate us. But I agree one must always be prepared for the worst. Last March Adolf Hitler spoke to an assembly of our officers and told them that their responsibility was not to what he called 'this lazy and decayed state'—he meant the republic—but to the German people who were yearning for release from parliamentarianism, and so on. I'm happy to say he did not get a very good reception. I consider it our job to do whatever we can to strengthen the resolve of our officers to resist such lures."

"How can you do that?" I asked.

"A systematic program of lectures and educational programs," the general responded. "The main point has to be that the Reichswehr is above politics. It is its sacred task to serve the state and to prevent the existing cleavage between classes and parties from ever widening into suicidal civil war. I know that our officers understand this and I have not the slightest doubt that if Adolf Hitler tried to do again now what he attempted to do in November 1923 and try to stage a coup d'état, the Reichswehr would crush him in twelve hours. After all, the precedent has been set. In the days after the collapse of 1918, the young republic could rely on the armed forces to defeat Bolsheviks and their friends and restore law and order very quickly."

"But instead of using such crude tactics as a coup d'état," I said, "Hitler has now allied himself with Alfred Hugenberg to defeat the Young Plan. Isn't there considerable danger that this time he will win by playing politics?"

"Oh, I don't think so," Schleicher shook his head with a tired smile. "Their petition doesn't have a chance in the Reichstag. They'll soon split up. This is a short-term *mariage de convenance*, nothing more. Hugenberg is a romantic dreamer who is out of his depths in the real world of power politics. A large majority of Germans won't swallow all this talk about the enslavement of the German people. Nor will they condone attempts to embarrass President Hindenburg, just because he has allowed himself to become a symbol of Weimar."

"Oh, I haven't heard about that."

"In the original version of their petition, Hugenberg and Hitler demanded that any agent of the state who signed treaties with foreign powers be accused of treason according to paragraph so-and-so of the constitution. They knew very well that the head of state signs many such treaties. They knew what they were doing. If a few sensible people had not insisted on revising their petition and the bill had passed, it would have meant that President Hindenburg could be tried and found guilty next time he signed a treaty, and sent to prison."

The clear implication was that von Schleicher was one of those sensible people.

"General," I asked, "have you read *Mein Kampf?*"

"Oh, I've looked at it," he said, as though he had just tasted something he did not like. "I'm afraid I can't take all that myth making very seriously. But, as I say, one must always be prepared for the worst. The coalition government has already begun to disintegrate. Once the economy collapses, the parties may not be able to agree on a new government. The President may have to govern by decree, according to Article 48 of the Constitution. I do not consider that the end of the world, by any means."

"But surely it can't go on forever."

"It can go on until reasonable people begin to understand that, unless the system is changed, extremists on the Left or on the Right will take over. I have submitted a plan to the President that has not been published, and that should not be published as yet, though quite a lot of people know about it. I have no objection at all to you conveying it to your president in confidence."

"You have my word, General."

"I would be happy to send you a summary to your hotel. But let me tell you now what it's about. Very simply, I propose a new political combination, government by a cabinet composed of men unhampered by considerations of party loyalty, governing from the standpoint of the national interest alone, appointed by an elected president and relying upon his support. The cabinet would be responsible to the president and not to the Reichstag, which, however, would play an important advisory role and in which the opposition parties would have their say."

"You're describing a system not very different from the one before November 1918. Except that nobody elected the Kaiser."

"Exactly," said the general, a faint smile on his lips. "At the same time I am developing ideas about allocating to unions a very important and well-defined role in the state and establishing a system some have called 'Prussian Socialism'."

I pondered this for a moment, wondering whether I should make a light-hearted comment. No, I thought, that would probably be unwise. I was, of course, familiar with his line of thought. It reminded me a little of Mussolini's ideas, which have considerable following on Wall Street, even though before the war he had been editor-in-chief of the socialist newspaper *Avanti*. Herbert Hoover, of course, has always found Mussolini's views repellent. As have I.

I decided to strike a different note.

"Suppose a man who at first seems perfectly all right is elected president," I said. "But one morning people wake up to discover they've elected Adolf Hitler."

Von Schleicher laughed.

"You certainly have a lively imagination, Herr Hammersmith," he said. "Then there will always be members of this club"—he waved to his fellow officers in their armchairs—"who will throw him out."

The Record

In 1930, 1931 and 1932, as the economic crisis deepened, Kurt von Schleicher pulled his strings. First he disposed of Chancellor Hermann Müller, a *social democrat, then Heinrich Brüning, of the Catholic Centre Party, whom he had first promoted to follow Müller. Brüning's successor was Franz von Papen, who appointed von Schleicher Reichswehr Minister. In December 1932, after von Papen's fall, he succeeded at last in having President Hindenburg name him chancellor.*

Von Schleicher made a determined attempt to seek support from the unions to stop Hitler and implement Prussian Socialism. However, he did not have time. He was outwitted. In January, 1933, after some hectic manoeuvring, President Hindenburg was persuaded to invite Hitler to succeed von Schleicher as chancellor.

On June 30, 1934, during the 'Night of the Long Knives,' six plainclothes S.S. men drove up to the general's villa on the Wannsee and shot down both him and his wife.

16

DIE GRÜNE KATZE

After seeing von Schleicher in the Scharnhorst Club, Peter took a taxi to the Kurstrasse entrance to the Reichsbank. He hoped to be alone for a few hours to take notes on his conversations with Paul Levi and Kurt von Schleicher and have a rest before going out again to have a quiet dinner somewhere. Then he would proceed to Die Grüne Katze [The Green Cat], the new political cabaret he had heard about.

He was thwarted.

Brigitte, in a state of high agitation, was waiting for him at the door. Now, what had been Horst Zahlendorf's threat? That if he saw her again, he would not return to America alive? Well, now Peter had seen her again.

"I have to speak to you." Brigitte's voice was hoarse with excitement. "May I come in?"

Peter rang the bell. The uniformed, gold-braided valet appeared.

"This is my friend Fräulein Kerner," Peter announced in the manner of a field marshall. "I vouch for her."

The man was used to taking orders.

They took the elevator to the second floor. Peter said nothing. Obviously, he thought, Zahlendorf had told her about his visit three hours earlier, disclosing Peter's whereabouts. Zahlendorf had probably explained to her the reason why Peter felt safer in the Reichsbank that in the Adlon. They entered his suite. Brigitte took off her hat and coat and threw herself on a chair. She wore a light blue dress with a very short skirt.

Once again, Peter found himself facing the familiar conflict between Desire and Principle, this time with the addition of a large dose of Anxiety. It was, however, not large enough to diminish—at least not for more than a second or two—his burning desire to spend another night of love with her, possibly after *Die Fledermaus* tomorrow.

But what was the Principle involved? That according to the most elementary requirements of friendship he owed a duty to Charlie Chaplin to wire him immediately Brigitte's name and address, whether or not she was a stormtrooper's moll?

"Do you realize," Peter asked, "that by coming to see me you put my life in danger?"

"Why?"

"Your friend told you where to find me. Is that all he told you?"

"No. He told me a lot. But I don't care whether you're Jewish or not. I've broken up with him. I'm never going to see him again."

So that's why she had come, to tell him that she was on his, Peter's, side, not on the stormtrooper's.

Should he believe her?

Excerpt from Peter's diary

<u>Thursday, October 31, 1929</u>

In three days' time, I thought, my affair with Brigitte will come to a natural end. The important thing now is to make the best of it while it lasts, even if I can't trust her. After all, one can never be entirely sure about anybody, man or woman. At a strategic moment I will convey to her Charlie's question. She will most certainly be on the next boat to Hollywood. But when is that moment?

There is another question to resolve. Where will we go after *Die Fledermaus* tomorrow? Where is it safe for us to make love again, undisturbed by Horst Zahlendorf and his friends? Here?

Well, yes, here. Why not? This is probably as safe as any place, especially if I inform Hans Bräutigam and Egon Martens in advance. They will keep Horst Zahlendorf out, as well as any other invader. Making love to a millionaire in the Reichsbank is bound to give Brigitte a special thrill. True, there is some danger of running into Hjalmar Schacht or his wife Luise (in curlers?) on the elevator or in the corridor, since they lived on the floor above my suite, but I can handle that.

At this stage I will not go back to the Adlon. Perhaps I will risk it on Saturday night after I've written my report to the President and sent it off. Surely I may assume that any potential attacker will not take the trouble to kill me after I've done my job and am on my way out of Berlin anyway. Also, checking out of the hotel in the morning will be much simpler if I've moved in the night before.

Brigitte was pacing the floor.

"What's this?" she shouted. "A telegram from Charlie Chaplin?"

I had left it on top of the desk. While pacing, her eyes caught the words 'Greetings Charlie.' Who could blame her? She picked up the telegram in a delirium of excitement. Fortunately, her English was not good enough for her to grasp the content at a glance. Except for the words 'Louise Brooks.'

I decided in a flash that this was not the moment to translate the full text for her. Tomorrow, after *Die Fledermaus*, was the strategic time, depending on events between now and then.

"He's asking me to find Louise Brooks for him," I lied.

"Oh, do you want me to track her down for you?'"

"That might be a good idea," I said. "But don't do anything about it yet. Let's talk about it tomorrow. Are you coming to *Die Fledermaus* with me?"

"I've told you I would."

"But that was before your friend's visit."

She looked at me. I could not make out what went on in her mind. Suddenly I had an idea.

"May I suggest something," I announced. "You told me you're not going to speak to your friend again. But could you please go home and write him a note telling him that my Munich friend Putzi Hanfstaengl has arranged an interview for me with Adolf Hitler for next Tuesday. And if your friend says Hitler would never give an interview to a Jew, tell him I'm not a Jew and that I'm in Germany on a special mission for President Hoover. If he doesn't believe me he should check with the American embassy."

The Record

Ernst 'Putzi' Hanfstaengl's mother was a relative of the Civil War general John Sedgwick whose statue at West Point graces the United States military academy. Putzi's father was a prestigious art book publisher in Munich. Putzi was sent to Harvard in 1905 to study art history. There he met F. D. Roosevelt, T. S. Eliot, Walter Lippman and Robert Benchley. Before the war, he also knew Charlie Chaplin. He stayed in New York during the war, to look after the Hanfstaengl art shop on Fifth Avenue. After the war he returned to Munich and fell under the spell of Adolf Hitler's hypnotic oratory. Putzi was one of those who, like Frau Bechstein, introduced Hitler to Munich society and tried to teach him manners, for example not to wear brown shoes and black trousers. An excellent, very loud pianist, Putzi played Wagner for Hitler through the nights. He soon noticed an uncanny relationship between the ebb and flow of Hitler's speeches and Wagner's music. In 1924, he published the Hitler Song Book.

Once Hitler came to power, Putzi became Chief of the Foreign Press for the Nazi Party. But he soon fell out with Hitler and some of the other leaders. He was spared during The Night of the Long Knives in 1934 because he happened to be in New York. In 1937, fearing for his life, he fled to London. Like Bernhard Weiss, he was interned during the war as an enemy alien and, unlike the police vice-president, who was interned for only a relatively short time, Putzi was sent to Canada, where he remained behind barbed wire. In 1942, his Harvard friend FDR arranged with the British authorities to have him transferred to the U.S., where, after a stay in Fort Belvoir in Virginia, he was sent to a well-guarded villa called Bush Hill, near Washington. There, he analyzed Nazi propaganda for the U.S. government and wrote a psychobiography of Hitler, which FDR allegedly labeled 'Hitler Bedtime Story.' In the spring of 1946, he returned to Germany, in shaky health. He was kept in a camp in Recklinghausen for another six months before being allowed to return to bombed-out Munich. His son served in the U.S. army. In 1949, the Germans put him on trial. He was acquitted.

Putzi died in 1975.

• • •

Die Grüne Katze was in a cellar just off the Budapester Strasse near the Elefantentor. One of the favourite targets of satire around the Kurfürstendamm was the lunatics on the Right. So naturally Peter did not offer to take Brigitte along.

On previous visits to Berlin, he had seen most of the cabarets in the city and had nothing but admiration for their lofty political, literary, musical and theatrical standards—especially if he had a chance to hear lyrics by the great Kurt Tucholsky. Peter had hoped to meet Tucholsky again on this visit, but apparently he was not in town.

There was certainly nothing comparable to these cabarets in New York. Many of them were modeled on their counterparts in Montparnasse, with the walls in the lobby covered with sketches on menu cards, caricatures and signed photographs of celebrities. Though male performers like Werner Finck were memorable, Peter always thought the *diseuses* even more wonderful. His favourites were Grete Mosheim, Blandine Ebinger, Trude Hersterberg and the magnificently erotic Margo Lion. Fritzi Massary (Max Pallenberg's wife) and Claire Walldorf were great stars in larger theatres, but were not quite as much at home in these smoke-filled *boîtes*. And of course there was Josephine Baker, from St. Louis, Missouri, who had been a sensation in Paris where he first saw her at the *Folies Bergères*, wearing nothing but a belt of bananas, before she did the same in Berlin, at least as successfully. Having become the very symbol of jazz and everything new and exciting, Baker was unique and did not fit into any category. Last year Peter was amused to see that a Berlin publisher had brought out her memoirs, written at the age of twenty-two..

Excerpt from Peter's Diary:

Thursday, October 31, 1929

I entered Die Grüne Katze just before midnight. A heavily rouged boy, wearing purple lipstick, insisted on taking my coat. He said the first performance was to begin at twelve thirty. It was so dark that I had to grope my way to the bar. I settled down on a stool between a grandmotherly whore, amusing and *très sympathique*, who addressed me as *Süsser* [Sweetie] and said her name was Lottchen, and a man who looked at me and then, angrily muttering something unrecognizable, conspicuously turned his back.

I ordered two cognacs, one for Lottchen, one for myself. Then I did what I've occasionally done before on such occasions. I handed her five 100 mark bills under the counter. She looked at the money and gasped. Her usual price was probably 20 marks, or at the most, 30. Understandably not entirely certain what services were expected in return for this astronomical windfall, she thought she could not do wrong by regaling me with colourful vignettes from the Berlin underworld, including lurid stories about the booming traffic in cocaine. After a while I said I found these stories most enlightening and added, to clarify the situation, that I was certainly getting more than my money's worth. This relieved her so much that she planted a juicy kiss on my cheek, leaving a large stain of lipstick, which I didn't notice until, some hours later, I looked in the mirror when I was brushing my teeth.

A few couples—among them male and female couples—danced the Charleston on the stage.

At quarter to one the band began to play a noisy jazz version of the military march *Fridericus Rex*. By now the place was crowded. The MC, who identified himself as Rudolf Oberhoff, appeared. He stood in front of a backdrop of a fierce-looking green cat, painted, so it said in the program, by the daughter of Archduke Vladimir, a cousin of the late Tsar. Oberhoff wore the costume of the aged Frederick the Great, complete with three-cornered hat. Stooped over and leaning on his cane, he introduced himself as Otto Gebühr, the UFA actor who usually played him. Then he straightened up and chased the dancers off the stage with his cane. He took off his jacket, presented himself in a not very clean dinner jacket and welcomed us like a normal human being.

I made notes of the ten presentations.

1. A *Tourist Guide to Verdun*, performed by Eberhard Hertz, who praised the beauties of the moon landscape where the battle had been fought, demonstrating the triumph of Krupp and Schneider-Creuzot. Each had supplied both the French and the Germans.

2. A *Street-Cleaner's Wife's Rhapsody*, sung by Gerda Liebwald in the style of an interlude in one of Ernst Toller's expressionistic plays. She proudly displayed the Iron Cross First Class her husband had found in the gutter and brought home.

3. *Steambath*. Alfred Hugenberg and Adolf Hitler outdo each other as they dream up delectable tortures for the leading politicians of the republic. Sung by Oberhoff and the band leader, Kurt Meier.

4. *Stalin in Berlin*, performed by marionettes, to the music of the can-can from *La Belle Hélène*. President Hindenburg and his guests take

the salute at the Brandenburger Tor while the crowds cheer.

5. *I Know That My Redeemer Liveth.* Johanna Krug sings first a beautifully kitschy song about the lovely time she had with members of the general staff when the Kaiser was still Kaiser. Then, switching to Handel, she prays for his speedy return.

6. *Largo al Factotum.* Oberhoff, a.k.a. Figaro, explains the intricacies of the Young Plan to a board meeting of one of Alfred Hugenberg's media conglomerates.

7. *How to Make a Revolution.* Robespierre, Lenin and Ebert present short lectures. Robespierre recommends the guillotine, Lenin a sealed train to Finland Station, and Fritz Ebert Frederick the Great's Prussian Army.

8. *Lügen haben kurze Beine* [Lies have short legs]. A sermon on the old German proverb. Eberhard Herz impersonates the club-footed, undersized Dr. Goebbels haranguing his congregation on the virtues of absolute honesty. At the end Bernhard Weiss arrests him.

9. *Charlie at the Sportpalast.* Charlie Chaplin plays Adolf Hitler.

10. *Grand Finale.* Members of the cast dance the Charleston on the stage with anybody who wants to join them.

Notes

> "Now let me buy you a cognac, Herr Hammersmith." The man who had shown me his back turned to me after the show was over. I was amazed he knew my name. He offered me a cigar, which I declined. He had a severe stutter. "I've never before bought a drink for a millionaire."
>
> He signaled to the bartender. I noticed that he had only one arm.
>
> "I recognized you right away. I read the newspapers, you know. My name is Schildplatt. Heinrich Schildplatt. I've wanted to have it out with you ever since I saw that piece in the *Weltzeitung*. With your picture. Well, this saves me a visit to the Adlon. I want you to stop."
>
> He had an intense, heavily lined, memorable face, handsome but lop-sided. Somehow, he looked like an artist. His thick hair was grey and his hand was shaking.

"Stop what, Herr Schildplatt?"

"Predicting that Adolf Hitler will take over Germany."

"You don't agree?"

"It doesn't matter whether I agree or not," he said angrily. "I've no idea what's going to happen. Nor do you. All I know is that if he gets in there'll be another war. I've sworn to kill any person I catch saying that Adolf Hitler will get in. Prophesies like that are invariably self-fulfilling. If people talk about it, it will happen."

"Did you say 'kill,' Herr Schildplatt?"

"Yes, that's what I said. Kill. Nothing else works." He reached in his pocket, looked around, took out a revolver and put it back again. "This is not the only way I kill people," he explained. "The police have been looking for me for the last two years. Now let me tell you this. If you don't leave Germany within twenty-four hours you'll be next on my list. If you stay, you'll only go on saying that Hitler was the coming man to anybody you meet. You're suffering from the delusion that your warnings will open people's eyes. You could not be more wrong. They have the opposite effect. You've forgotten what Germans are like. Hitler will unleash World War Two. You'll unleash World War Two. Unless you leave town."

The waiter brought us our cognacs. I let him pay.

"Did you know," I asked, "that threatening people contravenes the German Criminal Code?"

"Paragraphs 240 and 241. I practiced law for three years before the war. Next question?"

"But now you're an artist, isn't that right?"

"Clever boy, Herr Hammersmith. Yes, now I'm an artist. I work with Paul Klee at the Bauhaus. And with Otto Dix. He says my corpses are absolutely life-like. I'm best with infantrymen who drowned in the mud. He says only people with shellshock get it right."

"How long were you in the mental hospital?" I asked.

"Only two years." He said this without the slightest hesitation. "While you, Herr Hammersmith, were making your millions."

"Have you read *Mein Kampf*?" I asked.

"Yes, my friend," he said, with dead seriousness. "It so happens I have. I'm the only person in Germany who understands what the man is saying."

17

EINSTEIN

Peter had met Albert Einstein once, at a banquet during Einstein's first visit to New York, in the spring of 1921. It was the day after Einstein and his wife were driven in a procession down Fifth Avenue, preceded by a huge poster that proclaimed 'This is the famous Professor Einstein,' while airplanes droned in the sky. Photographs of the scientist's face had been everywhere, the face of a sage and a saint, of a transcendent scientific genius, soon to be almost as famous as Charlie Chaplin's. The spring of 1921 was only two and a half years after the end of the war and Einstein spoke German.

The banquet had been held in the St. Regis Hotel and was given by a distinguished Zionist, whose name Peter could not remember. The purpose of Einstein's visit had been to help his travel companion, Chaim Weizmann, the president of the World Zionist Organization, who was also a scientist, raise money for the Hebrew University in Jerusalem.

At the banquet, Einstein had told his admirers how he was amused by the procession. Surely it would be more entertaining, he had said, to look at an elephant or a giraffe than at an elderly scientist. Peter hadn't liked his use of the word 'elderly.' At the time Einstein was forty-two, only five years older than he.

When Peter telephoned him on Tuesday to tell him about his mission for President Hoover and ask for an appointment, Einstein surprised him when he said he remembered the occasion when they had met perfectly. He told Peter he would be delighted to see him on Friday at ten, at home in his apartment at Haberlandstrasse 5 in Wilmersdorf, not far from the Pommersche Strasse where Peter grew up.

Einstein had another thing in common with him. As a boy, he had felt uncomfortable in the Kaiser's Germany. But instead of merely falling in love with Wedekind's Lulu as an antidote to the official stuffiness—as Peter had—Einstein took more drastic action. He was fifteen when he left Germany for Switzerland, renounced his German nationality and became a Swiss citizen. In 1913, by then a world celebrity after his world-shaking scientific breakthroughs, he accepted a research appointment in Berlin at the Kaiser Wilhelm Institute and the Prussian Academy, not because he had changed his mind about Germany but because he wanted to work with some of the most dazzling scientists in the world, men such as Max Planck, Fritz Haber, Walter Nernst, and Max von Laue.

Unlike most scientists and scholars, in Germany and elsewhere, Einstein was a pacifist. Therefore, once war broke out in August 1914 he was untouched by the war fever. Indeed, he opposed it consistently and openly, as did Bertrand Russell in England and Romain Rolland in France, and never had any doubts about the outcome. Already then Einstein considered himself a citizen of the world, not of any one country. Throughout the twenties he spoke his mind on many public issues.

His apartment was filled with solid old family furniture, probably much the same as that in the apartments above and below. However, his taste in clothes—open shirt, threadbare jacket, baggy pants, no socks, sandals—was not likely to be replicated.

The sofa in the living room faced two large double doors that opened to the music room, where he practiced the violin whenever he could, usually playing Bach. He also played chamber music with others, baroque music, Mozart and early Beethoven. Peter did not ask him whether the story everyone told was true—that once, when he and Artur Schnabel played sonatas together and he lost his place, Schnabel snorted, 'Albert, can't you count?'

Notes

We first made small talk about the tremendous fuss made all over Germany last March at his fiftieth birthday when he was celebrated as a national hero. The municipality of Berlin, knowing of his passion for sailing, had presented him with a villa near the Havelsee. Laundry baskets filled with telegrams and truckloads of parcels had arrived in his apartment, he said, some of them containing expensive presents from people he had never met. His wife gave them away. All that adulation, he said, was completely beyond his comprehension, though perhaps it was better to hero-worship a scientist than a general or a football player. It seemed to him that the republic was really celebrating itself. Perhaps, he said, one day the event would be observed as some sort of high point in the history of the Weimar republic.

"That sounds," I observed, "as though you were a pessimist about Germany."

"Not at all," he replied. "By no means. Of course I am worried now that Gustav Stresemann is dead and there's no successor of comparable moral stature in sight. But nowadays in Germany there are always enough men of good will in the wings who will step on stage, sometimes only at the last minute. No, I would not at all call myself a pessimist about Germany."

"I'm very pleased to hear you say that, Professor Einstein. I always thought it was your pessimism about Germany that made you a Zionist."

"No, not at all, it's not as simple as that," he replied. "I became a Zionist in 1914, when I returned to Germany. That's when I discovered that I was a Jew. I'd hardly noticed it before. It was not the Jews but the gentiles who taught me. Some of them, here in Berlin, in leading circles, displayed a chauvinism and a xenophobia that really surprised me. I had not met it before. When I went to school in Munich, I don't remember ever having come across anything like it. But I would not say that this discovery in 1914 made me a pessimist about Germany as such, not at all. In this respect I think there's no difference at all between Germany and the rest of Europe. For many, many reasons, which mostly have to do with the unpopular Jewish habit of thinking independently, I now regard latent anti-Semitism as a normal manifestation everywhere. This has convinced me that for us only the establishment of a national home in Palestine can cure the evil of hatred and humiliation to which we are exposed. Assimilation is not the answer."

"Surely this runs counter to the views of most of your Jewish friends."

"Yes, it does." Einstein's melancholy eyes smiled. "But they are used to unorthodox and uncomfortable ideas from me. I just think it's futile to ignore prejudice or, worse, open hostility. You simply can't argue with it. I think national borders and armies are evil, but that doesn't alter the fact that people need to live in national communities. The Jews in the old German ghettos were poor, they had no civil and political rights, they were insulated from what was going on in Europe. But socially they enjoyed an enviable spiritual equilibrium. Then the doors opened. Emancipation followed, but the feeling of strangeness between them and their hosts never vanished. By the way, you remember when we met in New York, when I came with Chaim Weizmann?"

"Of course."

"You know, I nearly didn't go. My friend and colleague Fritz Haber, also a Jew, begged me not to go. He said that anti-Semites would capitalize on my going to America with Weizmann at a time when the Allies were once again tightening the screws on Germany. He said innocent Jewish students would be made to suffer. That made me hesitate, but after giving it a lot of thought I decided to go after all. I would not let the haters frighten me. The mission served a cause of historic importance. At a time when anti-Semitism was rife in universities in Europe, and particularly in Eastern Europe, it was important to find resources in the United States to establish the Hebrew University in Jerusalem where Jewish students could study in a friendly and congenial atmosphere."

Suddenly a thought came to my mind. Gertrud had told me about a friend of Walther Rathenau's who had said that Jews should behave as though anti-Semitism did not exist. I asked Einstein what he thought of that.

"I think it's impossible," he said. "It touches us too deeply. You mention Walther Rathenau. When he considered becoming foreign minister, he asked me for my opinion. I advised him against it, not because I thought his life would be in danger, but on the grounds that Jews should not play such a prominent role. It would merely sharpen the general resentment against us. Unfortunately, he did not follow my advice."

There was a pause.

"Have you read *Mein Kampf?*" I asked.

"I confess I have not, and I have no intention of reading it. I don't have to. Hitler is not the only man who says that Germany should be purged of the Jews. His kind of hatred is common among radicals, more so than among ordinary people. The war and its aftermath have radicalized so many. I followed Hitler's trial in Munich with great interest, after his attempt to make a putsch in 1923. But, if I may say so, from what you told me on the telephone, you are making too much of him. He is one of many. You can't argue with these people. But I don't suppose it did any harm to draw President Hoover's attention to him. If you're right and we're facing years of economic distress, he would probably get a lot of attention for a while, but he would sink into oblivion again as soon as economic conditions improve. Hitler is no more representative of the Germany of today than many other similar aberration. He is a product of something old and not an originator of anything new. You must not allow him and others like him frighten you."

"I doubt," I said rather feebly, "whether anybody can frighten Professor Einstein."

This was too silly a remark to deserve a reply.

18

DIE FLEDERMAUS

Peter had followed Max Reinhardt's career since he first saw him as a boy, when Reinhardt was a young actor imported from Vienna, in plays by Ibsen and Gorki. By the time Reinhardt had had his first success as a director, in 1905, in *The Midsummer Night's Dream*, Peter had already left Berlin. He never saw Reinhardt's production of Wedekind's *Spring's Awakening*, the play that had meant so much for him when he was a teenager. He would have liked to have seen the current production by Karlheinz Martin, at the Volksbühne on the Bülowplatz, with Lotte Lenya and Peter Lorre, who had played the pathological child murderer in Fritz Lang's film M., but there was no time.

By now Max Reinhardt was the man who, more than any other, had established Berlin as the theatre capital of the world. But he was also active in many other cities, including New York, where his greatest hit was, surprisingly, Tolstoy's *The Living Corpse*, mainly because of a virtuoso performance by Alexander Moissi. In the Soviet Union, his production of *Oedipus Rex* was a huge success.

In Reinhardt's productions, everything was subordinate to the personalities of the actors. He loved them, big names like Helene Thimig (whom he married), Elisabeth Bergner, Werner Krauss (the original Dr. Caligari), Fritz Kortner and Ernst Deutsch.

On one of Peter's visits to Berlin, Reinhardt once invited him to a rehearsal. Peter was impressed by the way Reinhardt always laughed when the dialogue called for a laugh, even though he knew the text inside out.

This production of *Die Fledermaus* at the Deutsche Theater, which the critics said Reinhardt had restored from being a home for the aged, was indeed stunning. While leaving the music untouched, Reinhardt had converted the operetta into a drama. He had simply gone back to the original play by Mailhac and Halévy, the authors of *Carmen* and many of Offenbach's operettas. It was from those two that Johann Strauss got the idea in the first place, half a century ago.

At the premiere the year before, in a preemptive strike to ward off the purists, Reinhardt invited Strauss's aged widow Adele to give her blessing. He seated her in the imperial box, from which she dutifully applauded. For this she herself received wild applause, not least because her name happened to be the same as that of the delightful chambermaid in *Die Fledermaus*.

Adele Strauss had survived her husband by thirty years. In Vienna they called her the 'Cosima in Three-Quarter Time.' (Cosima Wagner, the daughter of Franz Liszt, was still alive in 1929. She died in Bayreuth a year later, having survived her husband Richard by forty-six years.)

This production was the same as the previous year's, but it was the first time Peter had seen it. After the overture, the curtain rose on a wine garden, with chestnut trees in bloom, with Falke, the *deus ex machine*, seated at a rustic table, a dandy in a flowing cape, puffing a cigarette on a long holder, a happy smirk on his face. None of this was in the original version, as Peter remembered it. Suddenly lanterns lit up and threw their light on leaves that fluttered to the strains of a Viennese waltz drifting in from nowhere. Falke rose, tossed a coin on the table and started swaying to the beat, a few steps to the left, a few steps to the right, then with feet hardly touching the ground, danced with ever widening circles across the stage. None of this was in the original text.

Reinhardt had engaged the pudgy, spellbinding super-Viennese Erich Wolfgang Korngold to be the musical director. Gustav Mahler, Richard Strauss and Bruno Walter were among his predecessors. Korngold gave it his special touch. In the ballroom scene in the second act in the palace of Prince Orloffsky, he added Strauss waltzes from other sources, and a polka or two, and played some of them on the piano. As to the Prince, usually a *Hosenrolle*, a role played by a woman in trousers, Oskar Karlweiss played him unforgettably as a magnificently decadent Viennese *Trottel*, an elderly, lovable, superbly aristocratic ditherer.

Excerpt from Peter's diary:

<u>Friday, November 1, 1929</u>

The production was pure, exuberant bliss. Even if Berlin's Spree could never hope to rival the Blue Danube, Reinhardt managed to convey the spirit of the waltz-king's Vienna so authentically, so beautifully, that Arthur Eloesser of the *Vossische Zeitung* expressed his regret, his tongue firmly implanted in his cheek, that unfortunately the Treaty of Versailles made it illegal for Germany to annex—have an *Anschluss*—with Austria.

How wrong I was! The Weimar republic that could create the climate for such a life-affirming work of art, such *joie de vivre*, such an all-pervasive spirit of humanity, could not conceivably be doomed. After all, this meant something, this was not merely the achievement of one genius alone. It was a collective effort. Such exhilarating perfection could not have come out of nowhere—it was a health certificate, more telling than all that clever political talk I had been listening to.

And it happened just at the right moment to help me put everything in the right perspective. Tomorrow I will write my report to the President, and on Sunday morning I will be off.

• • •

Back to the beginning. Where was Brigitte? It was now ten to eight. Our appointment was for quarter to eight. The performance was to start at eight. Was she coming at all?

I was watching the people streaming in through the doors. They were already in a good mood. After more than a hundred performances, everybody knew somebody who had already seen it and had raved about it. In Berlin nobody asks 'Have you seen Shakespeare's *Hamlet?*' The question invariably is, 'Have you seen Max Reinhardt's *Hamlet?*' Thirty theatre curtains go up every evening, but there are only two names that matter—Max Reinhardt at the Deutsche Theater and Leopold Jessner at the Deutsche Schauspielhaus.

And who is the audience? The bourgeoisie is the audience, the middle class, the burghers. Without them, no theatre, no opera, no art—and no Weimar republic, even though, as Paul Levi told me, the workers had started it. Well, the bourgeoisie took it away from them, for which it will never be forgiven.

But that is only part of the reason, I thought, why it is so hard to find intellectuals, artists and writers (other than Thomas Mann) who have a good word to say about the bourgeoisie. The main reason is that a generation ago the intelligentsia rebelled against philistine Victorian stuffiness, as I did when I grew up in Berlin, and as Lulu did in Wedekind's plays. Members of today's bourgeoisie are vilified as superannuated upholders of yesterday's values.

The ideologues on the Right despise it because the bourgeois prefer going to the theatre to dying for the Fatherland, and the Marxists on the Left can hardly wait for history to put them on its ash heap to make room for the Dictatorship of the Proletariat. No wonder the middle class lacks self-confidence. Surely, a society without a self-confident middle class is in danger. Last year, when Bertolt Brecht's and Kurt Weill's *Threepenny Opera* made a sensation, it could only have been a death wish that made the burghers flock to the Theater am Schiffsbauerdamm to see themselves crucified.

Where was Brigitte? It was impossible to keep my mind off Zahlendorf's death threat. I wish I was like Einstein, who has probably survived many death threats and, I was sure, was not afraid. Political assassins normally target people who symbolize the causes they oppose. Einstein is a cosmopolitan, a pacifist and a Jew. Compared to him, what do I have to offer? America? High finance? At a time when everything American is in high fashion and Hitler is courting the super-capitalist Hugenberg?

Why am I so afraid?

It was now five to eight. The more I tried not to think about Horst Zahlendorf the less I was able to get him out of my mind. Obviously, I was suffering from persecution mania. With good reason. 'The only man who counts with her is myself,' he had told me. 'She'll fake anything to please a man she thinks can be useful to her. She'll do anything I say.'

No, no, no! This kind of thinking is madness! Surely the only immediate, sensible question I should worry about is whether she had conveyed to Horst Zahlendorf my ingenious lie about going to see Adolf Hitler on Tuesday.

Ah—there she was, carrying a large handbag—one minute to go before the doors closed. Rarely had I been so relieved, so delighted. She was enchanting, absolutely lovely. She threw her arms around me, shocking the unshockable Berliners with loudly proclaimed apologies, excuses and vociferous protestations of passionate love.

"Did you tell your friend about my Tuesday appointment?" I asked, my heart beating, as soon as we reached our seats in the orchestra, row five, centre.

"I wrote him a note. I told you I'll never speak to him again."

"What do you have in your handbag?"

"My toothbrush. After the show, are you taking me to your lovely refuge in the Reichsbank?"

"Yes, I thought you might find that mildly amusing."

"Just as I had hoped," she beamed as we sat down. "At last I'll have something to tell my grandchildren! Love in the Reichsbank!"

Before I could tell her that we were first going to have dinner at Lutter und Wegner, the pudgy Erich Wolfgang Korngold entered the pit, made his bow, turned around and raised his baton.

Notes

In the taxi down the Friedrichstrasse to the Französische Strasse Brigitte and I were laughing and joking as though I was twenty-five and we had already been drinking champagne—which we did, with considerable enthusiasm, once we were firmly seated at a corner table in the ancient Weinkeller of Lutter und Wegner. This was the place where the poet and composer E. T. A. Hoffmann had told his tales in the early part of the last century. After the first glass, I reached in my pocket, fished out the Charlie Chaplin brooch that yesterday her (former?) friend had so rudely tossed back to me, and returned it to her. For this I was duly rewarded by a passionate embrace. There was no need for me to tell her, after we had disengaged, that Zahlendorf had suggested I should give it back to Charlie Chaplin when I returned to America.

"Oh, by the way," I said casually, once we had ordered mock turtle soup, roast duck and red cabbage, "do you remember seeing that telegram from Charlie Chaplin yesterday?"

"How could I forget! Louise Brooks. He wanted you to

find her."

"Quite right. However, that's not really what he said. I didn't want to tell you. I wanted to wait for the right moment. Which is now."

The waiter filled our glasses.

"Yes?"

"You've been told you look like Louise Brooks. Right?"

"Right."

"Well, it so happens Charlie is making a film to be called *City Lights*. It will be his last silent film, he says. He's written the script. He's done the casting. Almost all of it. But for one small part he needs a type like Louise Brooks. What would you say if I suggested you? The shooting for *The Blue Angel* will be over soon, right? *City Lights* is a silent film, so language is no problem. I think you'd be very good. I'd of course tell him the truth, that you're my friend."

Brigitte's mouth was open. "Would you really do that for me?" she asked.

"Of course, I'd be delighted. I might even drop in on you in Hollywood. Unexpected."

"But promise not to be jealous if Charlie and I..."

After the roast duck and red cabbage, and after two bottles of champagne, we adjourned to the Reichsbank. I had given my guardians Hans Bräutigam and Egon Martens advance notice. They received us warmly.

Just as in every first-class hotel, the Reichsbank's maids had prepared the bed. Brigitte discovered—I had not noticed it—that the bed sheets sported the embroidered, intertwined initials H and L, standing for Hjalmar and Luise Schacht.

Germany's economic situation was indeed grave. The Reichsbank could not afford its own bed linen.

19

DAS ROMANISCHE CAFÉ

Peter and Brigitte rested in the morning and then drove by cab to the Romanische Café, the 'waiting-room of geniuses,' opposite the Kaiser Wilhelm Memorial Church, at the corner of the Budapester Strasse and the Tauentzienstrasse. Brigitte proudly wore her Charlie Chaplin brooch. Peter had not yet been there on this trip. Anybody between Reykjavik and Tahiti, so it was said, who wanted to be anybody in the arts had better be seen there from time to time. It had not existed in his day, when the Bohemians met in the Café des Westens, otherwise known as Café Grössenwahn [Café Megalomania] on the Kurfürstendamm, corner Joachimtaler Strasse. That institution had expired in 1915, a victim of the war.

"Peter Hammerschmidt," a familiar baritone behind him called out, "don't be such an American snob. Come over here right away with your lovely lady and join the common people!"

Peter turned round and had the most pleasant surprise of the trip. It was Kurt Tucholsky, who he had been told no longer lived in Germany but only paid occasional visits. Peter was delighted at his extraordinary good luck— he would, after all, be able to hear the views of this intelligent, sophisticated, fearless observer of the dark, ugly side of the German psyche, just in time. He had not yet begun composing his report.

Peter was shocked to see how tired and drawn Tucholsky looked, how much he had aged. He was probably not yet forty and tried to conceal his increasing corpulence by wearing an expensive, made-to-measure suit. He had moved to Paris about five years earlier to take up the post of correspondent for the intellectual and influential weekly, the *Weltbühne*, for which he wrote regularly under four *noms de plume*—Peter Panter, Theobold Tiger, Ignaz Wrobel and Kaspar Hauser. He had felt acutely depressed in Germany and asked to be sent to Paris. But then, a couple of years later, when the editor, his friend Siegfried Jacobsohn, died Tucholsky was asked to take over. He returned to Berlin and stayed for about ten months. That had been the last time that Peter had seen him.

Tucholsky was a superb journalist, feuilletonist, witty, combative, versatile, prolific, excellent with dialect, especially Berlin dialect, a gifted poet, often moving and tender, sometimes sentimental, also a skilled, amusing novelist. He had a large public, including the young. Above all, he was a moralist who stood up for the oppressed, for the outsiders and the forgotten, and, in particular, since he was trained in the law, for the powerless victims of injustice, particularly for those who languished in Germany's archaic prisons.

'*Ein einheitlicher Mensch*' [a human being made of one cloth] was the phrase Franz Kafka used to describe him. In Tucholsky's essay "The Institution," which Kafka himself might have written, he used a prison as a paradigm for society as a whole, divided between the few who govern, who were the only ones who had freedom of choice, and the rest.

Tucholsky had seceded from the Jewish community in 1911 when he was twenty-one, explaining later that he did so, not out of opportunism—under the Kaiser life was easier for a Jew, he said, than for a man without any religious affiliation—but because from early childhood on he'd had a deep aversion to rabbinical sanctimony. He hated it when Jews shamelessly aped the worst characteristics of the German bourgeoisie. Peter remembered him saying once that the trouble was not that Germany was being polluted by Jews (he used Wagner's nasty word '*Verjudung*'), a common complaint of the anti-Semites, but that the Jews were becoming *boches*. From Jewish Germans he expected a higher standard of conduct than from non-Jewish Germans, and it was a constant source of acute anguish for him that so often they did not live up to it.

Die Grüne Katze thrived on his chansons. Gertrud occasionally sent Peter copies of the *Weltbühne*. Peter had also kept in touch with his books. He knew Tucholsky was by far the most consistently popular of the many excellent authors publishing in Germany.

Tucholsky had his first success in 1912, when at the age of twenty-two he published the romance *Rheinsberg*, which, as he once told Peter, had served as a manual for young lovers ever since. He often said about his political writing, 'Yes, I know I'm successful, but I'm totally ineffective.' But he did not really mean it; otherwise he would not have risked his life every time he attacked the enemies of the republic, many of them well armed. A scathing picture book of his, Deutschland Deutschland über Alles, with devastating photo montages by John Heartfield, had just come out. It was selling well and was being savagely attacked by the Hugenberg press and by Goebbels' Angriff, which called it an 'infamous assault on the German spirit.' Other Nazi papers sarcastically thanked him for dissecting the Weimar spirit so effectively that he was doing their work for them.

Three little marble tables had been put together near the buffet, so there was no difficulty for Brigitte and Peter to squeeze in.

Excerpt from Peter's Diary:

<u>Saturday, November 2nd, 1929</u>

I am making this entry after dinner in my room at the Adlon, probably the last entry during this trip. Brigitte had a rehearsal at four thirty in the afternoon, which gave me plenty of time to dictate my report to the President. I had pretty well worked out in my head what I was going to say. The embassy sent over a secretary who would see to it that it was sent by diplomatic pouch directly to the White House. Before dinner I had my things packed at the Reichsbank, spent half an hour on the telephone to Gertrud and wrote a note of thanks to Hjalmar Schacht. I will spend my last night here with Brigitte, before departing by train to Paris in the morning. As I mentioned before, I've decided the risks of staying here are minimal. I assume the news has been passed around that, thanks to 'Putzi,' I'm to have an interview with Adolf Hitler in Munich on Tuesday. That's all there is to it.

Notes

I introduced Brigitte to Tucholsky as a UFA actress, with a lovely role in von Sternberg's new movie. The world would soon be able to admire her.

"Peter Hammerschmidt has always had superb taste," Tucholsky said as they shook hands. "I've always envied him."

He turned to me.

"So you've come to seek refuge in your native Berlin from the crash on Wall Street. How wise of you. Don't worry. We'll look after you."

I gave him a mock bow and said, "It's good to be among friends."

Tucholsky was too civilized to make of fun of me as a plutocrat. He himself had had a comfortable family background, considerably wealthier than mine. His traumatic experiences in the war and his bitter disillusionment in 1918 pushed him far to the Left, though he had always been opposed to communist extremism and dogmatism. He was a good friend of Ernst Toller and was now a regular contributor to the *Arbeiter Illustrierte Zeitung,* which was close to the Communist Party. He urged his fellow intellectuals to find common cause with 'proletarians' against the common enemy. But no one knew better than he that if ever the proletariat actually proclaimed a dictatorship, as they said they would, he would fight it to the end. Tucholsky was a melancholy, depressive loner to the core, temperamentally the opposite of the sociable Bertolt Brecht, whose enormous talent, he said, made him 'feel small.' At the same time, men of the theatre worked in teams, which made it easy for them to steal from others and live off one another. As—so he said—Brecht did.

A myopic elderly gentleman with thick, horn-rimmed glasses who was somehow connected with the movies sat across the table from Tucholsky. He spotted Brigitte's Charlie Chaplin brooch.

"Charlie Chaplin?" He practically put his nose against it. "How come you're wearing this? Do you know him?"

"No," Brigitte beamed. "But Peter does. And I hope to meet him soon."

"Really? Are you on your way to Hollywood?"

"That's not impossible." She gave him a sunny smile. The myopic man again bent over the brooch. "Are these real jewels?" he asked.

Brigitte answered truthfully.

He began to reminisce.

"I also know Charlie," he said. "Or rather, I met him once. Maybe some of you people did, too, when Charlie was in Berlin in the summer of 1921, on his European tour. Am I the only one?"

He was.

"His films hadn't been shown here during the war. No doubt a few people remembered him from his pre-war shorts. But not everybody. Not the people at the reception desk at the Adlon. They had no room for him. His friend, a former newspaperman and a kind of manager who made all the arrangements—I happen to remember his name, Carlyle Robinson—was going to find another hotel. But at the last minute somebody in the lobby did recognize him and summoned Herr Adlon himself, who, full of apologies, offered him the royal suite.

"That evening, Charlie and Robinson visited a nightclub. I think it was the Palais Heinroth. The two of them were given a dim table in a corner. But Al Kaufman happened to be in the club, the big shot from Hollywood—you may remember him. He was the German representative of Famous Players Lasky. He saw Charlie, and so did the spectacular Pola Negri, who was with him. Of course, all eyes were on her. You see, she was the only real star we had at the time. She was very, very Polish. She had been a dancer at the Imperial Theatre in St. Petersburg and acted on stage and screen in Poland before Reinhardt invited her to Berlin, before the war, to play a big role in the pantomime *Sumurun*.

"She asked Charlie to come over. She could not speak a word of English and called him 'Jazz boy Charlie.' She had a rich handsome business man with her. Charlie was totally charmed with her and paid her extravagant compliments. The rich man was quite annoyed but felt he had to be polite. So he asked Charlie why he was always playing a tramp. 'If I was tall and handsome like you,' Charlie replied, 'I would not have to do that. You see, there would be no need for me to hide.'

"Later, in Hollywood, Charlie and Pola Negri had an affair. Both talked about it later in very different terms. But they agreed that they had fallen in love that evening in Berlin."

The myopic man turned to Tucholsky. "Kurt, I'm surprised you didn't meet Charlie."

"No, I never did. I would have liked to because of *Shoulder Arms*, that marvelous film of his. I saw it in Copenhagen two years ago. It was made in summer of 1918, while the war was still going on. The best anti-war film I've ever seen. As far as I know, it's not been released here yet. After all, the High

Command, with Hugenberg's help, remains firmly in charge of our movie theatres. They wouldn't like those scenes on the parade ground to be seen here, with Charlie lampooning the drill sergeant, even if it was an American drill sergeant. Nor the sequence in the trenches with Charlie jumping each time a grenade landed nearby. When he couldn't open a bottle he held it up so that Krupp, that's what he called the enemy, could shoot off its neck. When he couldn't light a cigarette, he lifted it up so that Krupp could do it for him. And that scene when everybody got letters from home except for Charlie! He looked over the shoulder of a soldier who did get one, laughed when the soldier laughed and was sad when the soldier was sad, until the man noticed it and slapped his face. Later, thanks to Charlie, they captured the Kaiser. The over-all effect of the film was not a bit anti-German. It was anti-war, that's all. That's why Hugenberg and the others won't let us see it. You know Charlie well, Peter?"

"I see him when I'm in Hollywood and he visits me occasionally in New York."

"And they correspond," Brigitte added.

I asked Tucholsky what he was doing in Berlin.

"I'm doing readings from my new book and giving lectures. Been all over the country. Have you seen it?"

"Not yet."

He opened his leather briefcase and pulled out a copy. I quickly leafed through it. There was a picture of a family of five in a crowded room in a slum— 'Never Alone.' Next, a montage of shiny new weapons. 'Where's Germany's money?' the caption read. This was followed by a picture of Prince Eitel Friedrich, one of the Kaiser's sons, in full uniform, a spiked helmet on his head. 'I'm a fat man,' the prince says. 'I don't give a damn for the republic. You'll pay. We'll stay.' Next, there was a page of photos of top generals in uniform, their chests covered with ribbons and decorations, over the text, 'Animals Are Looking at You,' the title of a popular picture book.

I passed the volume back to him. "You're in great form, Kurt," I said. "Congratulations."

"Thank you. They also liked it a lot in Cologne in March. So much so that, before I started my lecture, I received an

anonymous note advising me to get police protection, somebody was getting ready to 'give me a massage.' Last week I
gave a lecture in Wiesbaden. The Nazis decided to break it up.
I could finish it only after the police had thrown them out of
the hall. After it was over, some of them stopped a car and
pulled out a man and beat him up. They thought it was me."

"And still you carry on," I said, shaking my head. "I must
say, Kurt, I admire you."

I glanced at Brigitte. What was going on in her head? Her
face told me nothing.

"You're not going to return to Paris, Herr Tucholsky?" she
asked.

"No," he sighed. "Too noisy. I've decided Sweden is qui-
eter."

There was a pause.

"Have you read *Mein Kampf?*" I asked.

"I've looked at it, Peter. Pretty repulsive. Long-winded
and not very original. As a political strategist, Hitler seems to
be a bungler. It didn't seem to be very hard to put down his
putsch. I suppose Ludendorff wasn't much help. Why do you
want to know?"

"Because," I chose my words carefully, "I believe Adolf
Hitler will make history."

"You do?" Tucholsky was dumfounded. "I always thought
I had a monopoly in pessimism. Now you're trying to outdo
me. I'm not sure I like that. I'm so pessimistic that I can't live
in Germany any more. I know you left even earlier—when
was it? 1900?"

"1904."

"How old were you, if I may ask?"

"Twenty."

"Well, I left in 1924, when I was thirty-four. You beat me
by fourteen years. And now you're trying to beat me again, in
pessimism. I've been playing Cassandra since 1914. But Hitler? No, Peter. I think, frankly, this time you're going too far."

"Tell me what kind of disaster you're predicting."

"Where should I begin? The Kaiser's generals and their
supporters have never given up. For them, November 1918
has never happened. They behave as though their hands were
clean. They neither started the war nor lost it. I've been say-

ing this for nine years, ever since the non-revolution. Read my articles in the *Weltbühne*. I'm usually in it, every week, under one name or another. I said it a week before Rathenau was shot in 1922. I foresaw a right-wing putsch, to restore the generals formally to power. I presented a graphic description of the event, with all the gruesome details. Of course I assumed that Ludendorff would be involved. This appeared a year before he was actually involved, in Munich, with your man 'Adoof.' You may not know that when I speak of him I always call him that. ['Doof' is vernacular for stupid in German.] At the *Weltbühne*, we rarely consider him of sufficient significance to write about.

"Back to my scenario of 1922. The Rektor of the University of Berlin welcomed the new right-wing government. England tolerated it, to annoy the French. All those who resisted were killed, their graves, if any, unknown. Total number, 2,060. My friends have been saying to me for years, 'The times cry out for satire.' No, I reply. Should I satirize murderers? I wouldn't know how. I don't have the vocabulary. Like my friend George Grosz, I can only go after the judges, the prosecutors, the Junkers, the industrial barons and their hangers-on, the *nouveaux riches*, the old and the new generals who pay for them and who think of the republic as nothing more than a damned nuisance that will soon go away, an unpleasant little interlude. I need a cognac."

Somebody summoned a waiter.

"Back in 1925, around the time of Stresemann's greatest triumph, the Treaty of Locarno, when we made nice noises to the French and the British, I saw clearly what was going on behind their backs. In 1920 we had promised them that our Reichswehr was not to exceed a hundred thousand men. But it was obvious to the generals that in order to carry the war to a victorious conclusion at last, the war, may I add, they had begun so gloriously in 1914, they needed a few more than a mere hundred thousand men. So they made their plans accordingly. In 1925, I was living in Paris and I saw it all quite clearly. That was the year our venerable field marshall was elected President of the Weimar Republic, symbolizing precisely the opposite of Goethe's Weimar. All you had to do was look at Hindenburg's face and you knew what lay ahead. "

The waiter brought the cognac.

"The military planners," Tucholsky continued, "approached their task the way German comedies are plotted. The first two acts pose no great difficulties. But invariably, the problem is the third act. First, there will be an *Anschluss* with Austria. That will be the prelude. The next target is France. But, you see, this time the generals will be very, very clever. They figure there's no need to attack France. Much better to travel to Paris via Warsaw. So they attack Poland. This will go quite well. But the trouble is that in order to do this properly they have to make a deal with Russia. That won't be quite so easy because each thinks the other is cheating. Oh, I nearly forgot, they also have to take Czechoslovakia. Nothing to it. And so on, and on, and on. And of course in the third act they'll lose again."

"Oh no, not again," Brigitte gasped.

"I'm afraid so, mademoiselle. I said these things four years ago and I say them still. In March I did a reading on the radio, on 'The Day of the Book.' The Nationalist Party lodged a formal complaint against my appearance, on the grounds that I was the man who had written: 'Let us not celebrate those who were killed in the war. Instead, let us mourn them. They died for nothing. The enemy is not over there. The enemy is right here.' Because I'd written that, I should not have been allowed to speak on the radio. I was called un-German and who knows what else. But don't think for a moment that the people who lodged that complaint are the kind who would support a right-wing putsch now. Why bother? They've got everything they want without a putsch. They own the president, the civil service, the judiciary, the schools and the universities. And of course the military. Men like Hjalmar Schacht will soon play along with them, too—you'll see. They're all united in their common opposition to the republic. All the people they don't like they simply call Bolsheviks. There's no need for a putsch any more. The situation has become hopeless. I'm off to Sweden. Waiter! The bill, please."

The Record

In 1932, after having moved to Sweden, Kurt Tucholsky, in despair, ceased publishing and called himself an ex-writer. Troubled by deteriorating health and deep depressions, he continued writing letters to many friends which were subsequently published under the title Letters from the Land of Silence *they were filled with expressions of anguish about all the things he had not grasped, he and so many others. Nauseated with what was happening, he felt he had wasted his life.*

Tucholsky took poison and died on December 21, 1935, in a hospital in Göteborg. The last entry in his notebook was, 'If I had to die now, I would say, "Was that all?" And, "I don't think I understood things properly. Everything was a bit too loud."'

20

THE REPORT

Dear Mr. President,

For reasons I hope to be allowed to explain to you personally as soon as I return home, I've had to conclude my conversations after five days. However, I saw some of the best informed and most representative people in Berlin and think I can say that I've been able to obtain a fairly comprehensive impression of the state of opinion. I am grateful to Ambassador Jacob Gould Schurman for having given me excellent guidance.

This is a short preliminary report.

I have not changed my mind, even though of the eleven people I saw only two agreed with my view that the coming depression will ultimately enable Adolf Hitler to come to power, consolidate it, establish a brutal dictatorship and launch another war, unless he is stopped.

These two were both men of the Left, the playwright Ernst Toller, who is working with the free trade unions, and Paul Levi, a social democratic member of the Reichstag and a former collaborator of Lenin's. Levi believes that, given the right leadership, the two workers' parties, his and the communists, which together command a large majority of the votes, could stop Hitler, whatever Stalin says. This is a view not shared by Toller, who thinks the division between the two parties remains too deep to make this possible. He has no faith in party politics.

The others agree with you, in various degrees and for various reasons, that the republic is now strong enough to survive the coming troubles. May I add that you are in good company—your ambassador, Albert Einstein and my sister, Gertrud, who remembers you with respect and affection. They all share your point of view. So do two of my old school friends, the psychiatrist Teddy Lindhoff, who believes that serious conservatives would not allow a man like Adolf Hitler exploit their case, and Bernhard Weiss, the Vice-President of the Berlin police, who is confident that the republic can be successfully defended against both communists and Nazis.

The influential General Kurt von Schleicher assured me that the Reichswehr would most definitely not allow Hitler to come to power. He has worked out his own political blueprint, which is still confidential but which he authorized me to pass on to you. He, however, would preserve the republic in name only. He envisages an autocratic regime that by no stretch of the imagination could be called democratic. However undesirable to anyone who cares about freedom, it would definitely be better than Hitler and it would undoubtedly attract men like Hjalmar Schacht who are increasingly impatient with representative government.

I had one surprise. I saw the writer Kurt Tucholsky whom I admire greatly and whose writings I have enjoyed for many years. He is a man of courage and integrity. For him, the Weimar republic is in fact already a realization of von Schleicher's blueprint, a thinly disguised continuation of the Kaiser's Germany. I was sorry that he could not see that Hitler, who in my view understands mass society much better than Tucholsky, is not merely a right-wing demagogue and adventurer but a quasi-religious ideologue who may well have unsuspected talents as a political and military strategist. Tucholsky does not see that Hitlerism is a new phenomenon, not merely the repeat of something old, and he does not understand that a brilliant man totally without scruples like Dr. Joseph Goebbels, Hitler's man in Berlin, uses propaganda techniques that to some extent he copies from the world of commercial advertising and that would have been unthinkable in politics in an earlier period. One could even imagine that it was he, Goebbels, who gave Adolf Hitler the idea to wear a little black moustache in order to resemble Charlie Chaplin, a figure universally loved in Germany.

Like many others, Tucholsky attributes the fragility of Weimar to the events in Germany of late 1918 and 1919, when the new social democratic government, paralyzed by fear of Bolshevism, sought protection from the Army. To be more specific, the government, helped by the Army and by largely improvised paramilitary units or Freikorps, effectively prevented an indigenous German version of democratic socialism from taking root. In spite of my own capitalist convictions and practices, I also think that was a great tragedy. The Freikorps were often supported financially by naive, well-meaning anti-Bolsheviks, in and outside Germany, who are now mortified because so many of the their members became freelance murderers and supporters of Hitler.

I am sure that you, Mr. President, like many other Americans, are wondering whether there is any danger of the Kaiser coming back. Tucholsky, of course, thinks it would make little difference. My own impression is that among the common people in the big cities, the Kaiser is largely discredited, but not so among right-wing conservatives and, of course, the military. I've been told that for this reason Hitler takes great care to avoid any contact with him. He wants to appeal to the masses.

However, in small-town Germany there still is a good deal of nostalgia for 'the good old days.' I had the opportunity to experience this first-hand when by chance I listened to a remarkable broadcast. I will tell you about it when I see you.

The Weimar republic must be saved. It is the most democratic government that Germany has ever had and is a realization of the hopes and dreams of many decent Germans who did not share Bismarck's and the Kaiser's militarism. Even if it never had enthusiastic support outside intellectual circles, the republic's achievements in the arts and sciences within a mere decade have been astounding. Such achievements are a fair way, perhaps in the end the only truly reliable way, to measure the value of any society.

If the republic fails, the outside world would be almost as much to blame as the Germans themselves, because, for short-sighted though all-too human reasons, it never gave the republic a fair chance.

But it must not fail. Of all the old allies, the United States is best equipped to play a major role in alerting the world to the danger posed by Adolf Hitler. Should he assume power and unilaterally rescind the Treaty of Versailles or any of the international agreements his predecessors have signed, including the agreement to pay reparations—however reduced—the allies must immediately take decisive steps to force him to live up to these commitments, even if it means marching in and occupying Berlin. Such drastic measures are necessary until, with the help of decent Germans, the constitution is restored and the dictatorship crushed.

If I may say so, Mr. President, no one would be better suited to assume the leadership in this vital enterprise, if it becomes necessary, than a man of your moral stature.

I am looking forward to seeing you in a few days' time.

21

A LETTER FROM
DR. BERNHARD WEISS

The news of Peter Hammersmith's sudden death of a heart attack in Berlin on Sunday, November 3, 1929, just as he was about to leave for Paris, was reported on the front page of the *New York Times* and the *Washington Post*, and in many other papers. A file of obituaries and tributes was among Catherine Hammersmith's papers, together with the Berlin diary.

There was also a letter from Bernhard Weiss, dated November 15, 1929.

Dear Mrs. Hammersmith:

May I, first of all, offer you my most sincere condolences. The loss you suffer is indeed irreparable. As you may know, your husband was an old school friend of mine, one of the few really good friends I've ever had in my life, even though we saw little of each other in recent years. But he was never far away from my thoughts and I shall always miss him.

I know that Ambassador Jacob Gould Schurman has kept you informed on the course of events since November 3. In spite of your husband's prominence and the acute interest the press took in the circumstances of his death, we have been able to shield our police investigation from the glare of publicity and to stick to our official story that your husband died of a heart attack.

In fact, your husband was murdered. He died of poison in the last night of his stay in Berlin, the night from Saturday, November 2, to Sunday, November 3.

We have been extremely fortunate to have found his diary, which was of invaluable help in our investigation. He had already packed it in his suitcase. I am enclosing it in this shipment. Thanks to it, and thanks to the cooperation of a number of witnesses, we have been able to resolve the case in record time.

The diary contains references to four suspects who each had a plausible motive. However, we have been able to establish that the murderer was Heinrich Schildplatt, whom he met only once, in the cabaret Die Grüne Katze, on the night of October 31. It was Schildplatt's view, stated with great emphasis to me and to a number of other interrogators, that in order to save Germany he had no choice but to kill the man who was telling the world that Hitler would eventually succeed in assuming power. He was convinced that, unless he acted, your husband would consider it a matter of conscience to make this prediction to opinion leaders in the United States and in Germany, in the mistaken believe that he was ringing the alarm. But Schildplatt was profoundly convinced the effect of this prediction in Germany would be the precise opposite. It was bound to make it actually happen. It would turn out to be a self-fulfilling prophesy.

Schildplatt had an exemplary war record and won many decorations for exceptional bravery. In 1917, he suffered shellshock and was a mental patient for more than two years. Clearly he never fully recovered. We have been informed that his lawyers will plead insanity when the case comes to trial.

How Schildplatt or his agent made his way to your husband's room in the Hotel Adlon in the evening of November 2 and applied five milligrams of the lethal poison Monolit to his toothbrush has not yet been resolved. But there can be no doubt that he was the murderer. He has confessed. Large quantities of Monolit were found in his apartment.

May I say that I shall always reproach myself that the protection I provided was not able to save your husband's life. I assure you it was the best available. But obviously it was not good enough.

You may be interested to know something about the other three suspects we investigated.

One was the writer of the letter who referred to your husband's interview that appeared in the *Weltzeitung* of Monday, October 28. The writer stated that the age of slavery was over and that his Abraham Lincoln was Adolf Hitler. We were able to identify him as a retired professor of history who lives in Cottbus. We discovered that he had written several similar letters to others and never thought for a moment that anybody would take his threats seriously. He is being charged and will appear in court on December 15.

Second, Horst Zahlendorf. During the twenty-four hours before Peter's death he had been on leave of absence from his duties as bartender at the Hotel Siegfried in Lichterfelde and was on uninterrupted duty in his S.A. unit. He could not have done it.

Third, Brigitte Kerner. We took her into protective custody the morning of Sunday, November 3, while she was still in a state of severe shock. We released her on November 12, after we had obtained unshakeable evidence that it was not she but Heinrich Schildplatt who was the murderer. She is now *en route* to the United States for an important appointment in Hollywood.

May I assure you once again of my deepest sympathy.

Yours sincerely,

Dr. Bernhard Weiss

• • •

In his autobiography, published in 1964, Charlie Chaplin wrote about the genesis of *The Great Dictator*:

> War was in the air again. The Nazis were on the march. How soon we forgot the First World War and its torturous four years of dying. How soon we forgot the appalling human debris: the basket cases—the armless, the legless, the sightless, the jawless, the twisted spastic cripples...
>
> Alexander Korda in 1937 had suggested I should do a Hitler story, based on mistaken identity, Hitler having the same moustache as the tramp: I could play both characters, he said. I did not think too much of the idea then, but now it was topical, and I was desperate to get working again. Then it suddenly struck me. Of course! As Hitler I could harangue the crowds in jargon and talk all I wanted to. And as the tramp I could remain more or less silent. A Hitler story was an opportunity for burlesque and pantomime. So with this enthusiasm I went hurrying back to Hollywood and set to work writing a script. The story took two years to develop...
>
> Had I known the actual horrors of the concentration camps I

could not have made The Great Dictator. I could not have made fun of the homicidal insanity of the Nazis.[12]

NOTES

1. Mary Jane Matz, *The Many Lives of Otto Kahn*, Pendragon Press, New York, 1953, p. 236.

2. Emil Julius Gumbel, *Verräter verfallen der Feme: Opfer, Mörder, Richter, 1919–1929*, Malik, Berlin, 1929.

3. On August 26, 1920, the Catholic politician Matthias Erzberger, one of the signatories of the armistice, was shot at point-blank range at a resort in the Black Forest where he had gone for a rest. The two murderers were officers of a Freikorps who had false passports and escaped to Hungary.

4. The German government had declared that it was unable to make the reparations payments that were due. David Lloyd George, together with the French Foreign Minister Aristide Briand, recommended that a European economic conference be called. On April 10, 1922, the conference got under way in Genoa. The German delegation was led by Walther Rathenau.

5. Later, Pope Pius XII.

6. Ernst von Solomon, *The Outlaws*, Jonathan Cape, London, 1931.

7. Kenneth Tynan, *Show People*, Simon and Schuster, 1979, p. 269.

8. Tynan, *Show People*, p. 310.

9. Brigitte may have been wrong. Von Sternberg may have named his femme fatale after Lola Montez (1818–1861), the Irish-born adventuress who cost King Ludwig I of Bavaria his throne and brought disaster to her many lovers.

10. Edgar Jung, *The Rule of the Inferior*, Lewiston, New York, E. Mellen Press, 1995.

11. Harry Domela, *Der Falsche Prinz*, was first published by the Malik Verlag in 1927, and published again in 1979 by the Athenäum Verlag, Königstein im Taunus.

12. Charlie Chaplin, *My Autobiography*, Bodley Head, London, 1964, p. 424.

Québec, Canada
2000